Bobbit Rock

Joseph Landing

Paperback ISBN: 978-1-950282-72-2

Hardcover ISBN: 978-1-950282-73-9

eBook ISBN: 978-1-950282-74-6

Distributed by Bublish, Inc.

This book is dedicated to my mother and father.
Thank you for always believing in me.
I love y'all.

1. The Wretched Man

"Tell me about the Wretched Man."

Isaac Murphy slowly raised his head. His eyes burned with grief, sorrow and above all else... dread. He bore his burning gaze into the eyes of Dr. Adam Brady, who reflexively looked away, troubled by the vile emotions directed at him. Dr. Brady's lips quivered, as if uttering the mere words "Wretched Man," were poisoning his mouth.

Isaac flinched, and all the hatred disappeared. The fear was taking over. He shut his eyes tight and pushed through it. His shaking hands, restrained from asylum handcuffs, grasped tightly to the pant legs of his white jumpsuit, standard issue for inmates. His lips parted and he spat out the truth.

"The Wretched Man is the monster on my shoulders and the devil in my mind. I can't escape him. I can run. I can hide. But he will always be on my person, always in my shadow. His eyes will stare at the back of my head where I can't see him, but I know he's there. And everywhere I go, he comes with me, ruining anyone who gets too close. That is my curse."

"And why does he haunt you?" Dr. Brady asked.

"Because, I summoned him at the Bobbit Rock."

***

Dr. Brady scribbled the words, *Bobbit Rock,* onto his notepad with sweating fingers. Isaac flexed his shaking hands. His nails were rough, dirty and long. Isaac stared at them, disappearing into his own thoughts. Dr. Brady clicked his pen loudly, snapping Isaac from the daze. Dr. Brady took in Isaac's shabby appearance, a man ruined by regret. His sagging shoulders held the weight of all the grief and guilt he had borne since the death of his wife and child. His green eyes, bloodshot and exhausted, were tainted with fear. A scraggly beard crawled across his face and his jumpsuit hung over a gaunt frame. Beneath his left eye, was a zipper of stitches. The healing wound was still red and swollen.

"Take me back, Isaac, to the beginning. I want to know it all."

Isaac chuckled dryly at the request without taking his eyes off his own twitchy hands.

"Why would you believe me? No one else has, besides Emily... You all just swallowed what the government said and threw me in the locker, along with everyone else."

Dr. Brady set his notepad and pen on the ground and raised his hands.

"I'm all ears. Now tell me about the Bobbit Rock. Tell me about the Wretched Man. Tell me about... Emily."

A ghost of a smile crept across Isaac's face.

"Okay."

Isaac leaned back and closed his eyes as the memories of his childhood flooded forward. The bare interrogation room faded into the thick forests and rolling mountains of Appalachia. The sun shined on a gorgeous spring morning. Wind stirred the leaves of tall trees, and birds flitted about in the blue sky. A wide bike trail snaked through the woods and a group of kids on bikes could be heard peddling along it.

"I grew up just outside of Callahan, South Carolina. Every weekend and summer was spent riding bikes down mountain trails, climbing trees and fishing. There were a lot of kids in my little suburban neighborhood, so there was always something to do and someone to play with."

In his mind's eye, the kids picked up the pace, hooting and hollering with laughter and bumping each other on the trail. A young Isaac, led the pack.

"My mother and father passed away in an accident when I was twelve." His throat closed, even after all these years…

"It hurt."

The memory continued and behind young Isaac, a girl sped up and bumped him with her wheel. Young Isaac turned around and smiled, his sorrow washing away as the girl beamed back at him. She was blonde, with warm green eyes and a little chip in her front tooth, quite the tomboy.

"Emily sure was something, even back then," Isaac mused. Young Emily scooted past young Isaac with a burst of energy. Not to be outdone, young Isaac dropped a gear on his bike and took off after her, leaving the other kids behind. They raced along the mountain trail, gathering speed in the tight race. Young Isaac inched ahead, and young Emily put her head down to keep up. The tree line opened, and a shining lake came into view. The trail dipped towards the lake and the two kids headed downhill.

"She was a go-getter, a fighter," Isaac said. "We were always competing, to see who was the best."

Despite being smaller, young Emily had a lot of heart and was holding her own against young Isaac. With the water only moments away, the two took a deep breath and pushed forward with all they had.

Young Emily won by an inch. She jumped off her bike and held up her arms in victory.

"I let you win!" young Isaac exclaimed.

Young Emily rolled her eyes. Young Isaac walked up to her and took her hand. They stared into each other's eyes and smiled. The two kids leaned forward and shared their first kiss.

"I will always love her," Isaac whispered.

Isaac's memory darkened. In his mind, the sun disappeared as the kids faded away and darkness rolled across the lake. A storm blew in and driving rain soaked the landscape. The sound of heavy footsteps was heard as the deep black woods enveloped the world.

"The death of my parents took me to a dark place. I became reckless. Seeking out danger was how I dealt with his passing." Isaac faltered as more memories flooded back.

"When my parents died, Emily was all I really had." An ironic smile crossed Isaac's face as he stared at Dr. Brady.

"She became my rock."

The woods got darker and thicker in the memory. Heavy breathing filled the air as young Isaac sprinted through the thick underbrush, sending dirt flying from his shoes. His eyes were bloodshot and brimmed with tears.

"With my parents gone, I was put under the care of my elderly grandmother. I dealt with the pain by being foolhardy. Death had invaded my life. So, I was going to confront it."

"If only I knew then how much more I had to lose." Isaac's face was ashen, and his eyes were cold. Dr. Brady clasped his fingers and leaned forward.

"Go on. You can tell me. Tell me about the Wretched Man. Don't make me ask again."

Isaac closed his eyes and gritted his teeth.

"The Wretched Man is a classic Carolina folktale. At the highest point in the thick forest north of Callahan, there is a massive rock formation."

Isaac remembered the moment he first took in the awe-inspiring view of the Bobbit Rock. The giant boulder stood resolute and imposing in the middle of a dead clearing. No plants grew in the perfect circle of the clearing. Only pale dirt dusted the lifeless ground. Young Isaac glanced back at young Emily, who was holding his hand.

The boulder was split down the center, and smaller, razor sharp rocks littered the dirt around it.

"That godforsaken rock...."

The two kids stepped towards the Bobbit Rock. It loomed high into the sky, dwarfing them. The entire clearing hissed negative energy, raising the hairs on the backs of their necks.

"Everyone knows to stay the hell away from that rock. It's probably claimed dozens of lives over the centuries... every life but two." Tattered police caution tape dotted the clearing. A collection of crosses with names on them adorned the clearing as well.

"It's against the law to climb the rock because of the fatalities. But I wanted to face that danger. So, I went in the middle of the night. Emily tagged along to try to talk me out of it, except I could not be deterred, even when a storm blew in."

A flash of lightning ripped through the night sky, illuminating the eerie spectacle for just a split second. Young Isaac approached the Bobbit Rock with young Emily in tow. She was frightened, but he was entranced.

"I couldn't stop staring at that *fucking* rock. Emily just wanted me to be happy. Though I don't think she ever thought I'd actually try to climb it. When she realized I was serious, it was too late to stop me."

Young Isaac reached out to touch the icy cold stone. His fingers grazed the wet rock. Time slowed down and the storm could have been a million miles away. A deafening silence overcame him. In a trance, he put a foot up on the first glistening step.

"The legend goes that a frontier family built a house out in those woods in the early 1700's. One day their little boy, Bobbit, found the rock while out hunting with his father. He climbed to the very top. His father, noticing his son had gone out of sight, went to look for him. He found the clearing just in time to watch his son jump from the top to his death. The early settlers were very superstitious. They surmised that the rock was cursed by Satan. They believed that when God cast him out of heaven, he must have landed on the rock, splitting it in two. After that, it became his home. So, when little Bobbit made it to the top of the rock…" Isaac leaned forward and bored his eyes into Dr. Brady's.

"He saw the devil."

"And so, he jumped."

"Wouldn't you?" Isaac retorted.

Dr. Brady cleared his throat and shifted uncomfortably.

Isaac chuckled dryly. "The rock has claimed so many lives. You know the nursery rhyme that kids used to sing, right? God, my grandmother hated it. Would you care to recite the tune?" Dr. Brady didn't respond. Isaac shrugged his shoulders and started the rhyme.

Round and round the Bobbit Rock.
Got to get to the top.
Once you make it to the end,
The Wretched Man will be your friend!

The temperature in the asylum cell seemed to plummet. Dr. Brady half expected his breath to frost. He took a deep breath to regain his composure.

"Continue," he stated.

Isaac glared down at the ground.

"Emily touched the rock, too." Young Emily recoiled from the cursed stone in horror, stifling a scream. She shouted for young Isaac to come down.

Young Isaac glanced back at her but continued the climb. Young Emily pleaded with him and even pounded the stone, but young Isaac paid no attention to her. He wanted to face death. He wanted to see the devil. In his mind, that was the only thing that could soothe his pain. With tears streaming down his face and rain pelting him, he scaled the razor sharp and jagged stone.

"Nothing was going to stop me."

Young Isaac took it one step at a time. Although he was careful, his foot suddenly slipped, and he clawed wildly for purchase. His fingers found a knife-blade of a handhold and took hold of it. Blood immediately oozed from a slice in his thumb.

"Absolutely nothing."

Blood ran in wet rivulets down his arm and onto his face as he pulled himself up the unforgiving rock face. The pain from his cut made him falter and glance at the ground. No stopping now.

"By that point, I'd die before I gave up. Mom was dead. Dad was dead. What did it matter?"

"You mattered to Emily," Dr. Brady whispered.

Isaac gazed at him, sadly.

"I know."

Young Isaac remembered young Emily's terrified face, gazing up at him from the ground as he scaled the rock, already halfway there. He was exhausted and hanging on by a thread. A violent gust of wind buffeted him and he nearly fell as a tremendous clap of thunder shook the world.

"ISAAC!" young Emily howled. Young Isaac managed to hold on for dear life until the pounding wind calmed.

"My muscles were screaming at me. Every part of my body was begging me to go back down. But not my heart... I should have gone back... *I should have gone back...*."

Young Isaac was soaked and frozen to the bone. Cradling his injured hand against his stomach, he approached the Leap.

"The Leap is where everyone dies. You must jump the gap from the right boulder to the left. The face of the left boulder is as smooth as glass. There's no purchase at all, nothing to grasp, or grab onto. The rock is so tough that it can't be pierced with equipment and there's no way to throw a rope because of the angle."

Young Isaac stared at the sheer rock face behind him. He would have to push away from the right wall, turn 180 degrees and then what? What was he supposed to grab? It was a sheer face, with no crack or blemish anywhere to be seen. He, like everyone before him, would surely fall to his death.

"How did you make the Leap?" Dr. Brady asked.

"I gave it a sacrifice." Young Isaac held up his bleeding hand and rubbed the wound on the rock face in front of him. He drew a line in blood that trickled down.

"I jumped."

For just a moment, young Isaac was suspended in midair between the two halves of the boulder, with an over forty-foot drop onto razor sharp rocks waiting beneath him.

He made the midair turn and planted a foot onto the left rock face. Despite no holds, he clung to the rock and started skittering up like a spider.

"Impossible. You can't have made that jump," Dr. Brady insisted.

"I made it. But I don't really remember what happened after the jump. I just remember the top."

It was a flat little surface, no larger than a coffee table. However, it had just enough room to stand up on. Young Isaac rose to his feet and stood up tall. He was a pale silhouette standing atop that midnight boulder, lit by strikes of lightning. He raised his arms and shouted. His words were lost in the storm. Young Emily could only stare in awe, still gripped by fear. Young Isaac had done it. He had climbed the Bobbit Rock.

The small smile on Isaac's face faded into a grimace.

"I don't remember coming down the rock. One moment I'm at the top. Then I'm back with Emily." Young Emily took young Isaac's hands. He was in a daze and shaken.

"Did you see anything? At the top of the rock?" Dr. Brady asked.

"No. Not at the top…."

Slowly, Young Emily pulled young Isaac away from the Bobbit Rock, to leave. As she led him out of the clearing, young Isaac glanced back at the rock with dread, suddenly filled with the fear he should have felt in his climb. He shuddered as they reached the tree line and disappeared into the brush. When they reached the trail, they hopped onto their bikes. Young Isaac checked behind his back again but found nothing. The storm continued to rage, with bright lightning streaking the sky.

"He was behind me. I could feel his eyes," Isaac whispered to himself.

The two took off down the trail. Young Emily was disturbed while young Isaac was near catatonic.

"Check left. Check right. Check up," Isaac whispered. He winced and grinded his teeth.

"You know that feeling when you're being watched?" he asked Dr. Brady. "Imagine if that feeling never went away. Imagine someone was boring their eyes into the back of your skull, but you could never find him. You could never escape his gaze."

Safely out of the woods, the two kids silently peddled towards their neighborhood. Neither said a word. At the turn, they stopped. This was where they split up to go to their homes. Young Emily tried to say something but couldn't find the words. Young Isaac managed a fake smile before pushing down the peddles and taking off in the opposite direction. Young Emily stifled a sob and then headed off reluctantly. Young Isaac was now alone. He pedaled down the empty streets towards his Grandmother's house. Again, he felt the prickling sensation that he was being watched. He looked to the left, to the right, and above him toward the night sky, but there was no one to be seen.

"I could feel his eyes on me. It was as if he was sitting on my shoulders, looming above my head. But every time I looked, he would dodge just out of sight. I knew he was there: The Wretched Man."

Young Isaac peddled faster. Sweat beaded down from his forehead and his heart pounded. Meanwhile, Isaac wrung his hands as he told Dr. Brady, "God, he was right on me. I could feel him. The Wretched Man!"

Young Isaac burst into tears as he rode until his muscles screamed and his bike rattled.

"Had to go faster! Had to keep pedaling!"

Finally, young Isaac got home. He jumped off his bike and bolted into the house. He slammed the front door behind him and locked it shut.

"Home. *Safe.*"

He flicked the light switch, but the overhead lights did not turn on. The storm must have knocked the power out.

His grandmother approached him, worry on her wrinkled face. She clutched a flashlight with a shaking hand and wore a pale old nightgown.

"Isaac? Where have you been? Don't tell me you've been out in that storm at this hour! You had me worried sick!" Young Isaac hung his head, but embraced his grandmother, relieved to not be alone. As he did the power cut back on. The two breathed a sigh of relief.

"I'm going to bed," he said. He quickly made for his room and shut the door, locking it behind him. He undressed and got into bed. He pulled the covers up to his chin and stared at the lamp next to his bed. He reached a hand out to click it off, but hesitated. Instead, he withdrew his hand and tucked it under the covers. He laid his head back and stared up at the ceiling fan. He shut his eyes, but they immediately snapped back open. He sat up in bed, worried. The door to his closet stared at him. He hopped out of bed and opened the door, empty.

"Do you believe in God, Dr. Brady?" Isaac questioned.

"Yes," Dr. Brady answered immediately.

"Remember what I said about God casting Satan out of heaven?"

Young Isaac checked under his bed and found nothing. He reached into a cabinet and withdrew a little pocketknife. He clicked it open and hopped back into bed, but left the lamp on.

"But what if instead of just casting him out, God cursed him."

Young Isaac pulled the covers up to his nose and shivered.

"Confined him to the earth and forced him to walk amongst men."

Young Isaac's eyes darted left and right across his bedroom. Left. Clear. Right. Clear. Up. Clear.

"Forever." Left, clear. Right, clear. Up, clear.

"He can't die, but…." Left, clear. Right, clear. Up, clear.

"He. Never. Stops. Aging." Left, clear. Right, clear. Up, clear. Left-

The Wretched Man was kneeling in the corner of the bedroom. His face was buried in his hands. He was fully illuminated by the harsh lamp light. The Wretched Man's skin was like leather, weathered to jerky consistency from millennia of exposure. Parts of it had torn like tissue paper, with the skeleton fully visible beneath. His frail bones were glass, with broken pieces jutting out at hideous angles. Vile pus and viscous fluids oozed from hundreds of sores and infected wounds. Each breath was agony, a wheeze that rattled and sputtered in his collapsed lungs. He fought for every inhale and burned for every exhale. His face was still obscured beneath the gnarled fingers, with nails that had grown to grotesque lengths.

It is best that no one ever sees his face.

"You can beat him. Crush him. Stab him. Burn him. Shoot him. But he will never stop coming for you."

Young Isaac was frozen with fear. His eyes were as wide as saucers and a silent scream escaped his lips. The Wretched Man began crawling toward the bed.

"Living for him is agony. And the only way he can feel joy...."

As the Wretched Man crawled, his face sagged down to the floor like a fleshy appendage. Bones cracked and split as he slimed across the carpet. He lifted a skeletal hand, and his massive talons of nails pressed against the bedcovers. Those nails had never stopped growing.

"Is if others suffer with him." The Wretched Man heaved himself onto the bed in a horrifying display of snapping bones and tearing flesh. Black and green ooze dropped onto the sheets.

"He latches onto them, for life. Everywhere they go, doom will surely follow."

The Wretched Man shoved his face next to Isaac, and a piece of leathery flesh burst from the side of his throat with the effort.

"He whispered to me...."

Black rotted lips cracked back to show a mouth with black gums full of holes. The stench of sulfur poisoned the room as he spoke the words,

"YOU ARE MINE."

The Wretched Man pressed his face into Isaac's, and a blood-curdling scream rent the air.

BOBBIT ROCK

2. Callahan, Several Months Earlier

"This city is cursed."

A crimson sun pierced a blood-red sky as the final gasp of daylight disappeared from the skyline of Callahan, South Carolina. Contrary to the rest of the state, Callahan lacked a soul. Industrial plants polluted the air, crime infested the streets, and the color palette was a mottled grey. Whereas the coastal city of Charleston bustled with culture and history, Callahan focused on business. The Silicon Valley of the South was the nickname that residents had ascribed due to the prevalence of tech industries and manufacturing companies which had set up shop. The Palmetto River divided the city into two and served as the source of much of the industry what with its direct path to the Atlantic Ocean. On the north side of the river lay much of the industry and commercial infrastructure; while more residential neighborhoods resided to the south.

But this commercially viable city was overcast with gloom. Every pedestrian walked with a hurried pace, eyes trained on the ground, afraid of catching another's gaze. Grey faces disappeared in shadow and hushed voices whispered in the dark.

Suddenly a loud *crack!* broke the cycle. Immediately, a scream shrieked across the wind and every head whipped backwards towards an intersection. A young man, maybe 25, had fallen in a crumpled heap. His hair was a shock of ginger, almost as red as the blood pooling beneath his body. His chest had been filleted and various viscera and organs hung out of the cavity.

The elderly woman standing next to the corpse screamed again, oblivious to the spray of blood that had stained her skirt. She gazed up at an adjacent apartment building, where a window on the fifth floor was open.

"He just… jumped," she stammered to the onlookers.

***

Business was booming at Callahan Cemetery. Multiple funerals were being held concurrently in the light drizzle. An ashen faced minister turned his face to the sky in prayer and shut his eyes. "Our father, who art in Heaven…."

Away from the funerals and near a large oak tree, was a small family plot. Isaac slumped in front of Emily's grave. He pressed his forehead against the cold headstone, and tears spilled down his face. He embraced the stone with both arms and wept. How he wished he could be six feet below with her, forever. The inscription read:

Emily Riehl Murphy
March 18th, 1982 – January 26th, 2019
Cherished forever. Best Friend, loving wife and devoted mother.

And beneath it:

Samantha Murphy
Our beautiful baby girl. We will always love you.

There was no date for Samantha. She had never been born. They died three months ago. Isaac covered his face and wept.

***

The front door to the Murphy home swung open. Isaac, stone faced with eyes bloodshot, trudged in and shut the door behind him. He dropped his bag with a thud and shrugged his coat off onto the floor. He walked upstairs, passing by a small asymmetrical hole in the wall. He stopped in front of his bedroom. Turning around, he stared at the closed door at the end of the hallway. The house was dead silent. It was overwhelming how quiet the house was, a complete lack of life, save for one exhausted heartbeat.

Isaac approached the door and grasped the dusty handle. With a creak, the door cracked open. The beautiful nursery sat just as it had when Emily had left it, waiting for a child who would never come. There was a messy pile of cute stuffed animals by the crib, some still with the tags on. Emily had planned to arrange them in just the perfect way for Samantha, since the big day had only been a few days away.

As usual, Isaac couldn't bear to touch anything, instead he pulled his wallet out and withdrew a small photo of Emily. She was a beautiful southern woman, with long blonde hair and dazzling green eyes. Isaac fell to his knees next to the crib and curled into fetal position, staring at the photo. A rattle of thunder shook the windows as rain pattered against the glass. With the image of Emily in his eyes, Isaac drifted off to sleep.

Isaac's watch alarm buzzed at 6:00 a.m. He opened his crusty eyelids and the first thing he saw was Emily's face. That brought the smallest comfort. Slowly, he rose to his feet and stretched his sore back. He wiped the crust from his eyes and tucked Emily's photo back into his wallet. As he left the nursery, he paused to look back, grimly. He shut the door as quietly as possible, as if not to disturb a sleeping child, before walking to the bathroom. Once inside, he stripped off his clothes and stood naked in front of the floor to ceiling bathroom mirror, staring at the gaunt and ruined man that was his reflection. *"You can't keep living like this, Isaac."*

Isaac touched his pale chest and felt the breath exit his lungs. He shut his evergreen eyes and listened to his heartbeat. He counted to five and inhaled. He then counted to five again, holding the air in, before letting it out slowly. He ran a hand through his light brown hair. Several streaks of grey showed premature aging. They were new. He was only 36. He turned from his reflection and stepped into the shower. Moments later, hot water cascaded down over his flesh. He turned the water to near-scalding and let the heat and steam envelope him.

"I can still feel her touch," he thought.

Isaac held his arms out, holding the spirit of Emily. They stood in the water together and let the tears flow. Isaac buried his face into her breast, comforted by her heartbeat.

"I will always love you," Isaac murmured. He opened his eyes and found himself alone in the shower. With a single nod of acknowledgement, he began to wash himself without a word. After cleaning, he left the shower and approached his sink. He didn't even glance at the other sink next to him. He brushed his teeth and then moved to shave his weekend stubble. Running the razor over his face, he gave himself a clean shave. He combed his short hair and then went to his bedroom where he threw on a suit and tie that served as his uniform. He also slipped on a soft bullet proof vest over his undershirt. It was Kevlar and rated to stop anything up to .44 Magnum. He'd been a homicide detective for nearly ten years and only in the last two had he started wearing the vest.

He headed for his closet, not glancing at the perfectly made up bed next to it. Inside the closet, he opened the large gun safe and withdrew two firearms. The first was a Glock 21. It was solid black and felt like a block in his hand. With thirteen rounds of 230 grain hollow points in the magazine and one more in the pipe, it *should* get the job done. He holstered the pistol on his belt and tossed a few spare magazines into his jacket pocket. He then stood up and grabbed the second firearm, a standard issue AR-15 semiautomatic rifle, and slung it over his shoulder. Moving to the end table by the bed, he withdrew his badge and clipped it to his belt.

Suddenly, his phone rang. He trudged downstairs and picked it up. It was on three percent battery. On the line was his partner, David Miles.

"Yeah?"

"Skip the office. Got a jumper on the intersection of King and Main. Foul play, his chest is all tore up, looks like Ghost Killers."

"When is it ever not?"

"Not very often."

"This city is cursed."

"Pick you up in two minutes. Almost there."

Isaac hung up and headed to the door.

***

David and Isaac drove to the crime scene, crossing the bridge over the Palmetto River. Isaac scrolled through the department issued laptop with the day's information. David took a final puff on his cigarette and tossed it into his empty coffee cup. David was only a year or two older than Isaac and a tad on the heavy side. A true Carolina boy, he had a thick southern accent. He and Isaac had been best friends since childhood.

"Kevin's not renewing his lease. Landlord offered to cut his rent forty percent," David said.

Isaac didn't look up.

"Yeah?" he muttered.

David glanced over at Isaac, grimly.

"Kevin said he wouldn't have stayed if his rent was zero. He's going back home to Charleston."

Isaac sighed.

"Lot of people are doing that. Leaving. I know you're going to miss him."

"Yeah, I love my kid brother. But I don't blame him for wanting to leave. Hell, I should leave myself. Nobody wants to be in this city."

"But most of us are stuck," Isaac stated.

David cut a quick glance to Isaac.

"Not you."

Isaac glared at David.

"Sorry," David apologized.

Isaac cooled off and turned back to the laptop.

"I'm sorry too. I shouldn't have done that. But you know I'd never leave. This place is all I got. And I must find *him*," Isaac stated.

"And we have to find the Ghost Killers," David replied.

"If they even exist."

"They better, or we are well and truly fucked."

The car exited the bridge and slowed down in the city traffic.

"This place used to be so nice. Remember as kids when we'd go to the town center and have a couple brews behind the movie theatre? There wouldn't be a soul in sight," David commented.

"More like you'd have a couple brews."

"You were always the lightweight," David quipped.

Isaac's gaze darkened.

"Maybe I'm the reason this city went to shit," Isaac affirmed.

"Don't say that. You didn't have a thing to do with this."

The cabin was silent for a moment after that. David cleared his throat.

"Anyways," he continued, changing the topic. "Kevin's lucky he wasn't a homeowner. Otherwise, he would've ended up like me and Charlotte, stuck in a mortgage with a house that would sell for less than half what we paid for it.

"Even then, who's gonna buy? If you gave it away for free, I doubt even the squatters would move in." The men chuckled ruefully.

"Yeah, they're better off bumming a ride to Spartanburg and taking up shop there," David muttered.

Isaac glanced out the window at the somber faces of pedestrians walking down the city streets. It was quite the bleak sight. "You know, there's a mansion in my neighborhood. I passed it the other day on the way home. 6,000 square feet for 500k. Four years ago, it would have been over 1.5 million, easy." Isaac said.

David shook his head. "No chance. That shit's too expensive. Drop it to 150k and then we'll talk. If I'm gonna move to Callahan to get my heart torn out by the Wretched Man, I expect to not break the bank doing so." David started to laugh again but stopped. It was as if all the air had left the car. David coughed nervously and tightened his grip on the wheel.

"I don't believe in him."

Isaac closed his eyes.

"I know."

David flicked his turn signal for the final approach.

"Hey, why don't you come play poker with the boys and me tonight? Get your mind on something… brighter," David recommended.

Isaac looked up and smiled weakly.

"Sure."

***

Isaac and David approached the crime scene. Only a few onlookers were watching from outside the police tape. Murder had become so commonplace that the spectacle wasn't all that interesting anymore. It was just a part of life in Callahan.

A police officer greeted the two detectives with a blank face and tobacco breath.

"Not a pretty sight. They cut his chest up real good before he jumped. Just let us know when you want to go up to the apartment and we'll open it for ya," the officer said.

Isaac nodded at the officer.

"Thank you. Any witnesses?" he asked.

The officer pointed at a few of the onlookers.

"Got a statement from them, but all they saw was him after the fall. The grandma in the back said he jumped. However," he jerked a thumb towards a homeless man who was being watched by another officer, "he says he knew the guy. Good luck getting anything else out of him. He's just been babbling about the Wretched Man."

David rolled his eyes and pointed at the body.

"Isaac, could you ID the victim so we can get in touch with next of kin? I'll start the questioning." David lurched over to the homeless man with a grumble.

"The Wretched Man!! The Wretched Man!! I seen *him*!" the man stammered. David glanced back at Isaac.

"How many more you think we'll have this week?" he asked.

Isaac dug out a notepad and checked his tally.

"Well we were at ten last week. So, I'd say eleven this week."

"Welcome to murder town!" David shouted back. Isaac turned back to the officer.

"Thank you for the help." The officer nodded and stepped away.

"Murder town," Isaac echoed.

Two years ago, Callahan's murder per capita had begun soaring exponentially. The staggering murder rate had taken off in the most recent year, causing the media and country to take notice. With a population of less than 500,000, Callahan was averaging ten murders a week this year. That equated to a murder per capita of over 100 out of 100,000 if the rate continued through December. That would be nearly as high as Caracas, Venezuela. Last year, the start of the rise in murders, sported a murder per capita of 65 per 100,000.

Isaac approached the body, which was being placed on a stretcher. He glanced at the man's ginger hair as the EMTs placed him in the body bag. The Red Head's body was covered in stab wounds and abrasions. It looked like he'd been attacked by a tiger. He likely jumped to escape whatever was attacking him. The EMTs placed a cover over the ripped skin and organs so the traumatizing visuals couldn't be seen anymore. As the body bag was being zipped up, the Red Head's skull drooped to the side and Isaac saw the left cheek of his bloody face.

A vicious slash had sheared off the back of his left cheek, and his ear was gone. Isaac stumbled backwards as a rising tide of panic surged inside him. "*Dammit!*" Isaac staggered away from the crime scene and pushed through the concerned onlookers. He reached David's car and fumbled with the door handle, before collapsing inside the passenger seat. Gasping for breath, he tried to stop the panic attack from rendering him catatonic. "*Inhale. Count to five. Exhale. Count to Five.*"

"Dammit! Goddammit!" He saw the ripped cheek again in his vision, only this time it was Emily's. Isaac buried his face in his hands. He took a deep breath and managed to slow his heartbeat enough for the blood to stop rushing in his ears and his face to stop burning.

The driver's door opened, and David came in with a somber expression. He put out a reassuring hand and touched Isaac's shoulder.

"Hey, come on, buddy. Let's take a quick walk. Clear your head. Let them get the body out of here first. We can come back and finish our job once that's done."

Isaac took a deep breath and nodded. The two got out of the car and headed away from the crime scene. They stepped off main street and ended up on a mostly empty sidewalk. Callahan, once a rising city, was starting to look like a ghost town.

"The cheek?" David asked.

Isaac nodded.

"Just a coincidence," David surmised.

"I can't take this," Isaac exclaimed.

"Yes, you can," David said, taking Isaac by the shoulders. Isaac shrugged him off. "Don't close off to me," David warned.

Isaac turned his back to David and started to return back to the crime scene, but David moved in front of him.

"You ain't getting rid of me that easily, buddy." David leveled his gaze at Isaac. "I know the last three months have been beyond hell and I'm sorry. But closing off to the people who care about you isn't going to do you a damn bit of good. And talking craziness about curses and the Wretched Man is only going to screw you up even more. If this city is going to survive, it needs sane people to keep it from falling off the cliff."

"I just don't know if I can do this," Isaac whispered.

"Yes, you can. You made a promise to Emily. You can do this. Besides, you're the second-best detective on the team."

Isaac raised an eyebrow.

"Second best?" he asked.

"After yours truly, of course!" David said, smirking.

Isaac smiled and clasped hands with David.

"Thank you, friend."

"Any time. Now come on. We need to actually do our jobs. Plus, somebody else has probably died in the last five minutes so we're in high demand!"

"Maybe I will get drunk tonight," Isaac mused.

David grinned.

"That's the spirit!"

***

The Callahan Police Department Headquarters was, to put it simply, chaos. A few years ago, this station was a sleepy office of bored detectives and burnt coffee. But now, it was a buzzing beehive. Officers and detectives ran around, shouting and barking orders. Overworked assistants manned the eternally ringing phones. The press filled the hallways, desperate to get a statement from anyone who was willing to go on the record. A line, thirty people long, clamored in front of Chief of Police Bill Laramie's door, anxious to get a word with the man who had no answers.

In the basement below, the firing range was white hot. Every stall was doubled up as sweating officers sent hot lead through paper targets. Brass casings piled up on the floor in little mountains as bullets rained down.

Outside the station, the daily protestors filled the air with screams, chants and shouts.

"Save Callahan!" "Fire Chief Laramie!" "How Many More Must Die?!" "The Wretched Man Comes!" The yells could be heard even inside the Homicide Department.

While most of those detectives were sprinting to and fro like it was grand central station, a few sat with empty eyes and hearts, dejected. Like Isaac, they had reached the level where it all just seemed so pointless. Isaac glanced at the second hand of his watch. *Tick. Tick. Tick. Tick. Tick.*

David sauntered up to Isaac's desk with a plate of doughnuts and coffee. He plopped them down in front of Isaac with a smile. Isaac's nose crinkled at the delicious smell.

"Good afternoon, bud!" David greeted. He grabbed a blueberry doughnut off the plate and scarfed it down. While everyone else was freaking out, David had a calmness that never seemed to crack. He turned to the sullen Isaac.

"Come on, you love strawberry," David encouraged. He nudged a strawberry doughnut closer to Isaac, who stared at it like it was a bug that needed to be squashed.

"I'll force feed ya if I have too. I've got plenty of experience doing that thanks to Amy. She hates eating her veggies." Amy was David's four-year-old daughter.

Isaac grabbed a mug of coffee and gulped some down. As he did, his phone rang. He fished it out of his pocket. He listened to the other end and then turned to David.

"They don't have any more lockers to store the body in," he muttered to David.

"What else is new?"

"Take him to the secondary locale. Send me the autopsy results when they come in," Isaac said into the phone, before hanging up.

"I feel bad for his family. They're gonna have to drive out of town just to identify his body," Isaac said.

A couple detectives rushed past and the room started to clear out.

"What's going on?" David asked.

Isaac reached out and stopped a passing Captain Anthony York. York was a stocky fellow with a bald head and thin steel rimmed glasses.

"What's happening?" Isaac asked.

York shrugged. "Chief has to give a press briefing. It's going to be televised."

"Didn't he do one of those last week?" David inquired.

"Yeah, but a lot more people have died since then," York responded.

David and Isaac followed the line of detectives and officers to the large meeting room. The press, cameras and Callahan PD were all packed in like sardines. Isaac wondered if he'd even be able to take a full breath in due to how crowded it was. He glanced at a large board that was plastered with photos and information about the Ghost Killers. With nowhere to sit, Isaac and David leaned against a wall at the back to watch the show. Chief Laramie approached the podium. He was out of his league. For twenty years he'd been in charge of Callahan PD, and eighteen of those twenty had been unremarkable. But now....

Chief Laramie was overweight, bald and sweating profusely as he peered at the crowd. At 65, his heart wasn't doing so hot under the overbearing stress of policing the most dangerous city in the country. He gulped.

"Callahan is sick," he began. "Two years ago, our city was relatively crime free. But since then..." He shuffled nervously and seemed mesmerized by the piercing red light from atop one of the news cameras.

Officer Austin McCormick, a lanky rascal, coughed loudly to snap Chief Laramie back to reality. Chief Laramie shook his head and wiped a sheen of sweat from his forehead.

"So far this year, Callahan is on the rate to have the highest murder per capita in the U.S. And that's unacceptable. Unacceptable!" He tried to shout the last word but it came out weak and thin.

Isaac rubbed his eyes; this was a train wreck already. Chief Laramie cleared his throat and managed to muster some resolve.

"But the Callahan PD is doing everything it can to fight back. In the last two years, we have doubled the number of detectives and officers on our staff. Talented men and women from all over the country have joined because they want to help this city. We are working around the clock to bring the culprits to justice."

The Chief took a deep breath, starting to get into a rhythm. "A year ago, we concluded that Callahan's mass homicides were being orchestrated by a group the press had labeled 'Ghost Killers.' Last year, sixty percent of all murders in Callahan showed similar trauma, consisting of penetrating lacerations primarily to the torso and abdomen, leading to death by considerable volumetric blood loss. This had become the killers' modus operandi. What has made it so difficult to track down potential suspects is the lack of identifying evidence at the crime scenes. DNA is never recovered, nor are fingerprints. The victims are killed when they are alone 95% of the time and never in sight of closed-circuit cameras or other recording devices. We are clearly dealing with professionals. Ghost Killers is a suitable name, since it's been so difficult to identify them."

A reporter stood up for a question.

"Chief Laramie, what did you mean by, penetrating lacerations?" the reporter asked. Chief Laramie grimaced and gripped the microphone.

"Well… You see-" A tabloid reporter cut in before the Chief could answer.

"Just tell 'em the true story! They got clawed apart! Shredded!" Chief Laramie cleared his throat.

"Well, yes. Generally, the victims suffer from knife wounds that resemble, animal attacks. But this is likely from the knives the Ghost Killers use and not anything like-"

"The Wretched Man?" a voice in the crowd asked. A commotion erupted as several people started shoving the one who spoke that name. Chief Laramie ripped off his glasses and stared daggers at the person who spoke that name.

"Who said that?! Who said that damn-" he paused, coughing awkwardly, after realizing that the cameras were still on him.

"Rest assured, Callahan PD will bring the Ghost Killers to justice. Until then, we recommend everyone in Callahan be smart and safe. Don't travel alone at night. Lock your doors. Be aware of your surroundings. Keep your head on a swivel. And if you see something, say something. That is all. Detectives, stick around because we are going to have a meeting."

The reporter spoke up again.

"Wait! What about the other forty percent of homicides? How come the suspects all say the Wretched Man made them do it?"

Chief Laramie pursed his lips.

"That is the end of the press conference. Please clear the room." The press reluctantly filed out into the hallway. Captain York stepped in front of the crowd and crossed his arms. Unlike the aging and deteriorating Chief Laramie, York still had some grit in him. He rested a hand on his scratched-up Glock 17 pistol, nestled in his hip holster.

"I'll keep this short, guys. Shit's bad and it's only getting worse," he said. "The feds are kicking down our door and if one more thing goes awry, they're gonna take over. We're going to have them policing the streets and running the show. Since Governor Randall declared a state of emergency, we thankfully have more funding, not that it's helped much."

York leaned forward with a stare that could cut steel. "The Ghost Killers have to slip up soon. We're going to catch one in the act, and this nightmare will be over. That's what I need you guys to do, catch one in the act. Find that lock of hair or fingerprint. Get one on camera. Or get information from one of the suspects we bring in. We just need one break and we can put this to bed and start healing. All of Callahan is counting on us, and we are not going to fail them."

York started to leave but stopped. He gritted his teeth and added.

"And guys, for the love of God please don't talk about the Wretched Man. That will get us nowhere."

Isaac felt an icy shiver run up his spine. Everyone in the crowd seemed to feel it too.

York rubbed his bloodshot eyes with a shaky hand.

"Get out there and find the Ghost Killers. Dismissed."

***

Isaac's dark silhouette filled the frame of his front door as he entered his dark home. He dropped his things and shrugged off his jacket before walking over to his living room and unholstering his pistol. He placed the pistol on the coffee table and turned to the kitchen. As he reached the fridge, his phone vibrated. He dug it out and checked David's text message.

"9pm for poker."

Isaac responded with, "see ya then." He tossed his phone on the kitchen counter and opened the fridge. He had 90 minutes before the game. It was time to cook.

Isaac was an excellent cook. It was one of his favorite pastimes. He'd taken culinary arts in high school and had spent many summers working in kitchens. For some time, he'd considered becoming a chef. He had planned so many beautiful birthday cakes for Samantha…

He pre-heated the oven before pulling out various ingredients from the fridge and pantry. He reached for the chef's knife and began to sharpen it expertly. The knife blade slid down the steel sharpening rod quickly and methodically. *Schink! Schink! Schink!* Isaac imagined slicing the jugular of the man who killed Emily. The man's ice blue eyes widened in terror as blood spouted from his throat and bubbled through his lips.

Isaac shook his head to clear his thoughts. He set the knife down and glanced up at the dining room table, where two empty chairs sat with full table dressings in front of them. An ornate mirror hung on the wall next to the table, reflecting the dining room and kitchen. Isaac looked at his image in the mirror and glanced at the empty space above him. He checked left. Clear. He checked right. Clear. He checked up. Clear. *"I'm alone."*

In front of one of the chairs, was a plate of untouched, spoiled food. It had been there a few days. A few flies were buzzing around it. A glass of white wine also sat untouched. Gritting his teeth, Isaac took the plate and glass and tossed the food into the trash before cleaning the dishes and putting them in the cabinet. He returned to the ingredients and prepared dinner. He withdrew the steak from the fridge and added a few more spices. He then peeled and chopped potatoes to prepare them for roasting.

As he worked, he disappeared into his own world and got lost in the art of cooking. The kitchen warmed from the heat of the oven and, for the briefest of moments, the house felt alive again as Isaac cracked a smile. As the bread rolls and potatoes roasted in the oven, Isaac seared the steak. With a hot cast iron pan, he placed the two steaks down in the sizzling oil. He threw in thyme, garlic, butter, salt, pepper and a dash of turmeric for that extra earthy taste. Meanwhile, asparagus steamed in a saucepan, turning vivid green and delectable. Isaac squeezed a lemon over them along with drizzled butter. He took his time with his craft, focusing on making the perfect meal. At last, he was finished.

He uncorked a bottle of Pinot Noir and poured it in two glasses, filling his nearly to the top. He carried the food and wine to the place settings. He lit candles and turned on the stereo. A tune with piano and strings filled the air. Isaac went to the empty chair and lifted a framed portrait of Emily that had been sitting on it. She was gorgeous in a red dress and smiling at the camera. Isaac placed the photo on the table in front of her chair and moved to his own. He clasped his hands.

"Dear Lord, thank you for the blessings you have bestowed upon us. We ask that you keep us healthy in mind and body and protect us from evil. I pray that you will watch over us as we continue this journey you have set for us. Amen." Isaac opened his eyes and looked at the photo of Emily with a warm smile. "How did you ever get me to be a praying man?" he asked with a chuckle.

The room remained silent. But Isaac cracked another smile and dug into his steak.

"Well, yes, it does remind me of childhood. Dad always made sure that we said a prayer before dinner. He said that Mom was big on religion, had him praying from their very first date!" Isaac buttered the bread roll and took a bite, delicious. He continued his conversation with no one.

"You know David and Charlotte's anniversary is coming up next week? And their little girl just turned four! I can't believe how fast she's growing. Time flies."

In the reflection of the mirror, Emily sat in the chair opposite Isaac, wearing the stunning red gown, pregnant and glowing. Her golden locks shone in the candlelight. She appeared only in the mirror, as if it were a window into the afterlife.

"Oh, I know," she said with a pearly smile, "I ran out today and bought Amy the perfect gift. I'm sure she'll love it… no thanks to you!" she teased.

"Hey, I was at work all day. I think it was thirteen hours!"

"That is awful, though I do miss working. Sitting around the house this last week has been so boring. But at least I'm getting everything ready."

"Yes, and it'll be perfect. Now… I think I deserve a reward for even remembering Amy's birthday, January 16th!" Isaac proudly exclaimed.

Emily chuckled.

"Babe. It's January 15th."

Isaac looked down at his asparagus.

"Well, shit."

Emily laughed and tucked into her steak. With a shining steak knife, she sliced a piece off, popped it into her mouth, and then closed her eyes in satisfaction.

"Dear Lord, so good. Honey, can you just make steak every day?"

Isaac beamed and puffed out his chest. "Gee, I don't know. I was planning on raising Samantha meat free."

Emily gasped over dramatically.

"Oh, absolutely not!" She smiled and raised her eyebrows. "Screw vegans," she whispered sexily.

Isaac wiggled his eyebrows.

"Then today, I am officially a vegan."

Emily bit her lip and squeezed Isaac's knee under the table.

"Oh yeah?" She moved her hand up his thigh.

He grinned, and the room seemed to fill with cheer and warmth. He drained his wine glass and took a few big mouthfuls of food.

"More wine, Emily?" Emily held out her wine glass with a flourish. Isaac grabbed the bottle from the table and poured some into her glass. The full glass immediately overflowed and spilled onto the white tablecloth, staining it blood red.

"Christ! Aw, I'm sorry!" Isaac started to dash for the kitchen towel, but Emily took his arm.

"No, no… it's okay. I'll just bleach it tomorrow. Don't worry about it."

Isaac felt a shiver and glanced down at his arm. Emily's hand was freezing. He shook his head, trying to keep the dream alive.

"Right. Okay. Um…."

"I looked around at Callahan Day Care today!" Emily cut in, desperate to change the subject to something happy.

Isaac shook his head again, dispelling his negative thoughts and smiling.

"Oh, yeah? How was it?"

Emily clasped her hands together, showing off her nice manicure.

"Just lovely. It'll be perfect for Samantha once I go back to work and she's out of my clutches."

Isaac chuckled. "More like out of my clutches. There's no way I'm letting her go. Not for a second!" he replied.

Emily crossed her arms with a frown and a glint in her eyes.

"Hey, now! I'm her Mommy!"

Isaac took Emily's hand across the table and gazed deeply into her eyes.

"I love you," he stated.

Emily squeezed back, her hand ice cold. "I love you, too."

She leaned across the table and he met her for a kiss, except he found only air. He opened his eyes to see she had pulled back to her seat.

"Babe?" he asked, confused.

Emily crossed her arms to ward off a sudden chill. Her bright smile had faded. "It's such a nice day care. I know she'll love it."

Isaac couldn't understand what had spoiled her mood. She was falling into a dark place.

"Babe?" Isaac reached out to touch her shoulder. He recoiled because her shoulder was hard, stiff and cold as ice. Isaac reached back and grabbed her shoulder, ignoring the freeze.

"I'm sorry! I just," Isaac stammered, blinking the cold sweat from his eyes.

Emily burst into tears.

"Emily? What's wrong?" He got up from his seat and moved to console her.

"Say something!"

Emily gazed up at him with watery eyes.

"She's never going to see the day care, is she?" she whimpered.

Isaac didn't understand. He looked down at Emily's very pregnant belly. "What? Of course, she will! We'll take her there as soon as we're ready! She'll love it. I'm sure.

"But what if she misses us?" Emily trembled.

"Well, that's okay because we'll always be there to pick her up at the end of the day. And if she gets too lonely... I'll leave work early!"

Emily shook her head. "You won't. You're always working," she stated darkly.

Isaac was stunned. He dried his forehead on his napkin.

"I... I must work. The city is falling apart. It needs people like me to give everything we have. It's the only way we can save it," he declared.

Emily looked down at her belly. "But what if one day you're not here, and I need you? Because the city is going to kill Samantha and I."

A loud *THUD* echoed through the house and the front door shuddered. A large crack split down the middle of the wooden frame. Isaac took Emily into his arms and embraced her fervently.

"No! I would never let that happen. I'll protect you and Samantha! I could never let anything happen to you two. I love you both so much. Nothing bad will ever happen; I swear to God." Isaac buried his face in Emily's neck.

Emily softly ran a hand through his hair, her eyes glued to the front door. "It already did."

Boom! The front door smashed open and a dark figure stepped into the house. Emily's scream pierced the air. Isaac didn't let Emily go. He held her as tightly as he could in between his arms as the dark figure lurched forward.

"No! I won't let you go. I'll never let you go," he whispered fiercely. The front door closed, and the dark figure faded away.

Isaac opened his eyes to Emily.

"You're safe, honey. You're safe. We're all safe."

Emily stared in horror at her flat belly. Isaac's eyes widened.

"What happened? Where's Samantha?" he gasped.

Emily reached under shirt and touched her navel where her child had been seconds before. Her eyes filled with fear. She tried to speak, but no words came from her lips.

Isaac shook her by the shoulders.

"Emily where is our daughter?!"

Emily recoiled in fear of Isaac. She withdrew her hand from her stomach, and it was drenched in blood. Blood ran in rivulets from a stab wound on her belly button. Her ear had also been sliced off. Isaac's jaw dropped at the trauma.

"Jesus Christ…. Oh, God!" Isaac pressed his hands against the stab wound on her stomach, trying to stop the bleeding.

"Please don't yell at me," Emily whispered. She collapsed into Isaac's arms. He laid her to the floor as his dream became a nightmare.

"Hang on, Emily! Please hang on! I love you! Please baby…."

Emily held out two shaking hands and took Isaac's face between them. "I love you," she whispered. Isaac blinked and Emily disappeared.

Isaac stood up and looked around the dining room. His gaze shifted to the northward facing window, in the direction of the Bobbit Rock. He tore his gaze away.

"Emily?" He swept the dining room but saw nothing. He began to panic.

"Emily?!" Isaac dashed over to the dining room table where Emily's food lay untouched. Her wine glass was filled to the brim and the luscious white tablecloth had been badly stained. Wine dripped down the table onto the floor like drops of blood. Isaac's eyes widened.

"No, baby… please don't leave me," he begged. Isaac grabbed the edge of the table and looked underneath but saw nothing. He spun around and wrung his hands in the air. *"Please don't leave me!"* Isaac grabbed her plate of uneaten steak and hurled it into the kitchen. It slammed into the coffee machine, shattering the glass pot on impact, and sending bits of china and glass throughout the kitchen with a horrific clatter. He seized the overflowing wine glass and slung it into the dining room window. It shattered and cracked the window. Isaac heaved the entire antique dining table into the air. It flipped and the food, candles and plates went flying. With a terrific crash, it all came tumbling down. The table groaned as the wood split on the hardwood floor.

Isaac screamed again and moved into the kitchen, smashing and swiping everything in sight. He grabbed the gleaming chef's knife and stabbed it mercilessly through the cabinets, screaming in rage, or perhaps, agony.

"Please calm down," Emily's pitiful voice cried out weakly.

Isaac froze in his tracks, the knife hanging limply from his hand. His fingers relaxed and the knife clattered to the ground amidst the rubble. He turned and embraced Emily.

"I'm so sorry, baby. I'm so sorry," he cried.

Emily's pained expression was blurry, as if seen through a veil. She wrapped her fingers around Isaac's and looked around at the wreckage. Isaac squeezed her fingers, so tightly that his knuckles were white.

"You won't let me go," Emily whispered, pained.

Isaac embraced her. "You're safe. I won't let you go, ever."

Emily bit her lip. "You won't… let me go," she repeated.

Isaac nodded his head. "I'll never let you go. I want to hold on forever."

"Oh Isaac…."

"What?"

"Don't ruin yourself for me. I would never have wanted that."

Isaac blinked, and Emily was gone once more.

Isaac stood there, alone once more in the house with nothing but his rage and his pain. Slowly, he raised his hands to his face, trying to remember what Emily's touch felt like. But he couldn't. Instead, all he could think of was the cold.

Isaac collapsed to the floor and covered his eyes. "*Why continue? What is the point?*"

In the rubble of shattered plates and appliances on the ground, Isaac withdrew the chef's knife. He gripped the wooden hilt and raised the now broken blade to his face. His green eyes stared back at him in the shining steel. Resolutely, he pressed the blade to the palm of his left hand and drew it slowly across the cushy pad between his index finger and thumb. Crimson blood welled up and ran down his forearm. Isaac pulled the knife away and again stared at his green eyes in the reflection, now marred by blood. The pain hit him, sharp and stinging, but it had no effect on him. He knew it hurt, but it didn't matter. He raised the blade to his throat, pressing the knife tip to his carotid artery, then froze.

"I don't deserve the easy way out," he sighed and dropped the knife to the side, before rising to his feet. He walked back to the dining room and approached the mirror. He stared at the bloody figure in the reflection. Isaac cocked his bleeding fist and slammed it into the mirror, shattering the glass into a thousand pieces.

"Agh!" This time he felt the pain, and it was brutal. Isaac cradled his shredded hand that was now bleeding heavily. Little shards of crimson glass were sticking out of his fingers. For a moment he thought he might black out from the pain, but he steadied himself and took a deep breath. "*Inhale. Count to five....*"

Isaac staggered outside to his car and got in, his hand slopping blood all over the steering wheel, despite the jacket he had hastily wrapped it. Another wave of pain rocked him, and he bit his tongue as a distraction. With his one good hand, he turned on the car and hit the road.

***

"Jesus, what happened?" the nurse asked, gaping at Isaac's hand, which still was punctured by shards of glass. A few large bloody splinters were hanging freely from the wounds.

"I punched a mirror," Isaac said flatly.

The nurse wasn't sure how to respond, so she just shook her head and got to work on his hand.

"It ain't the worst thing I've seen tonight."

***

It was 2 a.m. by the time Isaac returned home. His left hand was stitched up and wrapped in a cocoon of gauze. His right hand held a container of pain reliever. He popped some pills and glugged down some water before stumbling into the nursery. Exhausted, he laid down next to the crib, pulled out the photo of Emily, and closed his eyes.

***

In Isaac's dream, Emily searched her house for him. It had been a year since Isaac had climbed the Bobbit Rock. A violent storm raged outside, and all the neighborhood kids were watching a scary movie together, David was amongst them.

Thunder roiled overhead as Emily called out for her boyfriend.

"Isaac? Where'd you go?" she heard nothing but the pounding rain.

Emily's mother approached her from the hallway.

"Emily? What is it?" she asked. Emily shrugged.

"I can't find Isaac. He disappeared when the thunder started."

Emily's mother pointed upstairs. "I thought I heard some footsteps upstairs a few minutes ago."

Emily took off up the stairs and started searching through the upstairs bedrooms. She stopped at the closet in the guest bedroom and cocked her head.

"Isaac?" A quiet sobbing could be heard from inside. She creaked open the door and found him crying alone in the darkness. It was a pitiful sight.

"What's wrong?" she asked. He wiped his eyes.

"I got-I got scared."

Emily knelt next to him. He took her hands gratefully and squeezed them tight.

"Still scared of the Wretched Man," he whispered. Emily smiled and squeezed Isaac's hands back just as tightly.

"The Wretched Man can't hurt you, because I'm here. And together, we can take him." She said sweetly and kissed him. For that moment, they were just two young kids in love. Two heartbeats and two pairs of hands holding onto one another. When they parted, Isaac smiled and wiped his nose.

"You're right, we'll beat him together." They rose to their feet and started to head back downstairs, but Isaac stopped in his tracks. He grimaced and looked at Emily with pleading eyes. "You won't tell anyone that I was crying, will you?" he asked.

"Of course not, Mr. Macho Man," she teased.

Isaac rolled his eyes.

"Great."

***

In his sleep. Isaac smiled.

BOBBIT ROCK

3. The Red Head

*"Left. Right. Up. At least you can get a good visual of
your surroundings that way."*

Isaac awoke at dawn on the nursery floor. The first thing he saw
was Emily's picture. He had left a bloody fingerprint on it.

"Ah God...." Isaac flexed his hand, groaning from the pain.
"Dammit," he swore and shakily rose to his feet. Some blood had
seeped through the bandage and stained the carpet as well.

"Crap," he muttered. He walked to the bathroom and hopped
into the shower. After cleaning up, he changed the dressing on his
hand, wincing as he did so. He popped another pain pill and then
glanced at himself in the mirror. The utter exhaustion on his face
did not go by unnoticed.

He moved back to the nursery and retrieved the photo of
Emily. He tucked it back into his wallet and then went downstairs
to grab the portrait of Emily from the wreckage. He took that to
the bedroom and gazed upon the bed.

"Okay, Emily." He placed the portrait on Emily's side and
took a deep breath. He moved to his side and for the first time in
three months, got into the bed. He laid his head back on the pillow
and looked over at Emily's side. Her portrait looked back at him.
Isaac closed his eyes.

***

The distant ringing of his cellphone roused Isaac from his sleep. His bedside clock read 3pm. He'd slept most of the day. He glanced at the portrait of Emily and sighed. He then slowly got out of bed. He trotted downstairs and withdrew his phone from the debris. There were several missed calls and text messages from David. Averting his eyes from the disaster that was his kitchen and dining room, he raised the phone to his ear.

"Sorry I missed last night," Isaac began. Meanwhile, across town, David drove down the streets of Callahan on his motorcycle. His helmet featured a built-in speaker system that hooked up to his phone, allowing him to talk on the phone while driving his bike.

"No worries, man. I figured something came up."

Isaac glanced down at his bandaged hand and grimaced.

"So, what was it? Cause you didn't show up to work today. Chief's gonna be on your ass for that, especially given these… circumstances."

Isaac gently prodded his hand and winced. He reached for the bottle of pain pills.

"Yeah, I spent the night in the hospital, so I'm gonna head in with a good excuse. I'm also kinda loopy from the pain meds."

"Shit. Are you good? What happened?"

The passing asphalt reflected in the black lens of David's visor. Rain began to spatter the visor, so he slowed down for safety.

Isaac gingerly touched his hand, shaking his head at his own stupidity… and morbidity. "I had an unfortunate run-in with the mirror in my dining room."

"An unfortunate… run-in?" David asked.

Isaac cracked a smile.

"I punched the shit out of it."

"Well that's not healthy."

Isaac chuckled.

"Seriously, Isaac, I can't watch you destroy yourself every day. Please reach out to me when you are feeling low. I'm here for ya," David stated.

Isaac took a breath and considered David's statement. "Thank you. It's just… difficult. I don't want to let go," he breathed.

David gritted his teeth. The rain came down heavier and he took a turn. Callahan PD was just up ahead. He pulled into the parking lot and parked his motorcycle. He popped up his visor and pulled out a cigarette. "Losing someone you love… I'm so sorry you must go through this. But let us help you. We're gonna play poker again tonight. This time show up, you don't need two hands to play. I know you're not much of a poker player, but it'll be good for you. Anything to get you out of that damn house." David lit up a smoke and took a drag before heading inside.

"Okay. I'll come by. 9pm right?" Isaac asked.

"Yeah. Bring some brews. We'll have a good time. See ya in a bit. Oh, and York says he's assigning us a trainee, one of the new recruits he just hired."

Isaac's ears perked up.

"Really? Who's the unlucky man?"

David chuckled. "Unlucky *woman*! Grace Fletcher, young and apparently whip smart, still a boot though. We'll see how soon the city chews her up and spits her out."

"I'd be willing to put money on it," Isaac suggested.

"Please, you're the worst gambler I've ever seen."

"Is that why you insist I play poker? So, you can rob me?"

"Well…."

***

On Isaac's desk was a fresh stack of reports. It was the forensics and autopsy results of the Red Head. Isaac thumbed through the pages, scanning over the info.

"James O'Donnell, aged 25. Numerous broken bones and traumatic organ damage, death was by broken neck due to forty-foot fall," Isaac muttered. He moved on to the evidence and a grimace split his face.

"Goddammit." The results were as expected, absolutely nothing. There was no relevant evidence that could be used to identify a suspect. Isaac grabbed the file in a fury and stormed downstairs to forensics. He pushed through the door of the lab and approached one of the white coated scientists, a balding man in his early sixties with thick rimmed glasses.

"Nathan, you can't tell me there's nothing. You've got to give me something on the O'Donnell case." Isaac was near-desperate.

Nathan LeGris took off his glasses and rubbed his tired eyes. Deep dark circles hung under them. The forensics lab was a mess, and the press crowded the entrance. Scientists sprinted left and right with glasses askew and sweat on their brows. A woman in a white lab coat bumped right into Isaac, her arms overflowing with files and evidence bags.

"Sorry!" she exclaimed.

Isaac regained his composure and held up the O'Donnell file in front of Nathan's face. "It says clearly that there was an obvious struggle in his apartment before he fell. Hell, his lower intestines were hanging out when he jumped!"

"That's what the witnesses all said." Nathan said.

Isaac glanced again at the file. "Right, to escape whatever was attacking him. But in all that struggle, overturned sofa and bed, slashes on furniture, cuts on the wall, blood spatter, but no fingerprints, no locks of hair, no skin cells, no nothing that could identify the suspect?"

Nathan stared at Isaac blankly.

"Why are you questioning me like this out of the ordinary?"

Isaac lowered the file, his arms feeling heavier than bricks.

"Right... I just... hoped there might be something this time," Isaac bemoaned.

Nathan lowered his eyes. He reached out a hand and touched Isaac's shoulder reassuringly. "No, not this time. But soon. We'll find something. I swear to God." Nathan's comforting words were unfortunately hollow.

Isaac shook his head and looked Nathan over.

"When are you leaving?" he asked.

Nathan jumped a little. He cast a glance around to make absolutely sure no one else was listening to their conversation.

"How'd you find out?" he asked nervously, worried he might have let something slip.

Isaac waved away his concern. "It's only a matter of time for just about everyone here. We're losing people every day. I don't blame anyone who wants out, especially the folks with kids or are close to retirement. You planning on heading back to Pensacola?"

Nathan managed a small smile.

"Yes. Another month, and I'm putting in my two weeks. As the saying goes, I'm too old for this shit."

Isaac held out his hand and Nathan shook it. "Best of luck then for when you leave. Until then, help me out as best you can."

"Always, Isaac."

Isaac checked his watch. "Well, I've got to go speak to the O'Donnell family in ten minutes."

"More people wanting answers you don't have?" Nathan asked.

"Unfortunately, yes. And all I can give them is an empty promise." Isaac tucked the O'Donnell file under his arm and gave Nathan a nod before leaving the crumbling forensics lab.

As soon as he crossed the threshold into the hallway, he saw that Captain York was waiting for him. A smoldering cigarette hung from his lips as he acknowledged Isaac. York's shoulders were a little slumped and he was leaning rather heavily onto his gun holster. Next to York was a rather cute brunette in her late twenties. She had fair skin and warm brown eyes. She looked a little nervous, or maybe just excited to be working in murder town. She was Grace Fletcher.

***

"Detective Fletcher, this is Detective Murphy. He's one of the best men we have. You'll never meet a man who works harder than him," York stated.

Isaac extended his hand and shook Grace's. There was a stark contrast between Isaac's chapped and calloused hands to her professionally manicured nails, no varnish, but nicely shaped and shining. For a moment the handshake stuck, and the two met eyes. Grace found much in his eyes that frightened her. Past the cool façade of professionalism, there was a near hopeless emptiness behind his gaze.

Isaac shrugged. "Captain, I think that title belongs to you."

York chuckled dryly. "I just yell at people all day."

Grace put on a smile, trying to wash away the nervousness. "Detective Murphy."

"Isaac's fine."

"Right... Isaac. I've read all about you. Very impressive resume. The Blackhorn case? That was incredible," she complimented.

Isaac gave a side-eye to York. "The only thing incredible about that case was the fact that I didn't collapse from exhaustion after not sleeping for two weeks."

Grace chuckled nervously.

"But thank you. I'm looking forward to training you. We need all the help we can get," Isaac affirmed.

York cleared his throat and spoke. "I've got to go put out a dozen fires so y'all will have to continue the pleasantries without me."

York headed up the stairs, passing by David, who was snacking on a bag of kettle corn. David saw Grace and wiped his mouth with a handkerchief.

"Ah shit," he exclaimed.

Grace glanced over her shoulder and David straightened himself up while shoving the butter stained handkerchief into his pocket.

"And you must be Detective Miles! Grace Fletcher." Grace extended her hand and David wrapped his hairy paw of a fist around it. Grace's smile faltered when she realized her hand was now smeared with grease.

"Pleasure to meet you Detective Fletcher. Just David is fine. Uh... sorry." David downed the last few pieces of kettle corn as Isaac's phone vibrated. Isaac put it to his ear.

"Yep. We're on our way." Isaac hung up and looked at Grace.

"It's time to see one of the things that David and I do every day."

Grace's eyes widened. "Absolutely. What is it?"

***

Isaac, David and Grace consoled the grieving O'Donnell family. Mrs. O'Donnell cried into a stunned Grace's arms, and Grace started tearing up as well. Isaac and David, having performed this particular drill more times than they could count, were more or less stone faced. While Mrs. O'Donnell kept Grace busy, Isaac and David attempted to question a shell-shocked Mr. O'Donnell and the Red Head's young girlfriend. After several minutes, the inevitable demand for justice was made. Isaac, mustering up as much gusto as he could, gave an empty promise.

***

Later, in the homicide department, Grace had just finished setting up her desk, right next to Isaac and David's. It was after hours now, and the three of them were discussing job expectations. Despite it being "after hours," the place was still in pandemonium. Callahan PD never slept.

Isaac leaned back in his chair and sipped some piping hot black coffee. David propped his feet up on his desk and mulled over a new case absentmindedly, listening in somewhat to Isaac and Grace's conversation.

"If you don't mind me asking, how much did they sign you on for?" Isaac asked.

"75k, much more than I was making as a cop in Charleston. But I was hoping for more, given the… current situation. But I was ready to make the jump to detective."

Isaac scratched his chin thoughtfully. "Well, that's fifteen more than the starting salary was three years ago. Last year the city voted to increase wages to attract more detectives. It *should* be more, given that this is Callahan, but there simply isn't enough money. The city has lost significant tax revenue due to a mass exodus by residents and tourism tanking."

Grace leaned in quickly and puffed up her chest. "Well, I didn't come for the money. I came, probably like most of the other new recruits, because I wanted to have a legitimate impact on the world as a detective. I knew that Callahan was the city I needed to be in to do that. I want to save Callahan. I want to find the Ghost Killers and bring them to justice." Grace gave a confident smile as she finished. David golf clapped sarcastically, causing her to flush.

Isaac flicked a pen in David's general direction; it landed in his coffee mug with a splash.

"Oh, nice," David grumbled sarcastically.

Grace tried to wipe the grin off her face. Isaac chuckled and turned back to her. "That's very noble of you, and commendable," he said. "Not enough detectives in this department still have that passion. Most people are just looking for a way out."

Grace smiled warmly and Isaac reciprocated. David, fishing the pen out of his coffee, gave a snort in response. Grace folded her hands and turned to David.

So, what are you fighting for?"

"Paycheck," he muttered.

Isaac chuckled dryly. Grace frowned and asked him the same question.

So, tell me, what's your story? What are you fighting for?" Isaac receded a bit into his chair and Grace flinched, realizing she'd prodded a festering wound.

"I'm sorry! I didn't mean to pry."

Isaac waved her off. "It's alright," he said.

David glanced over at Isaac and held up his hand. "Now might not be the best-" David started, but Isaac waved him off as well.

Isaac took a deep breath and said the words quick to get it over with.

"I lost my wife and child just under four months ago.... double homicide. I want to find the man who did it." Isaac's eyes flashed darkly, *"and kill him!"* he thought to himself.

Isaac shook his head and collected himself for a moment, then repeated, "I want to find the man who did it. And I want to save this city. I made a promise. So, you and I have similar motivations, I suppose." Isaac tried a fake smile, but realized it was creepily cold and grimaced.

Grace touched his shoulder in apology.

"I'm so sorry, I didn't mean to bring up something so awful. If there's anything you need, let me know."

Isaac nodded. "Thank you, Grace. Let's not discuss this anymore. How about you? Charleston, huh? You grow up there?" he asked.

Grace smiled, happy to change the subject.

"I did! Born and raised."

"Downtown?"

"Isle of Palms. I love the beach. But, who doesn't?"

"I don't," he stated flatly. Grace stared at him. Isaac stared back. Grace cracked a smile while Isaac casually took a sip of coffee.

"Well, *most* people like the beach, Isaac," she said, continuing with her story. "I went to Clemson, majored in criminal justice and put in my years as an officer so I could make the jump."

Isaac finished his coffee and placed it down.

"Got any family around here?"

Grace shook her head.

"Just me. It was kind of spur of the moment. The position opened and I knew I had to take it."

Isaac's eyebrows bunched together.

"So, you just left your hometown to go live in the most dangerous city in the country, with no friends or family around?"

"Well, I was hoping to make some friends. And besides, it's only a three-hour drive to Charleston."

"Well, color me impressed, Grace."

David's phone started ringing. He pulled it out of his pocket and winced. "Shit," he spat.

Isaac glanced over.

"Something wrong?"

David's face flashed with pain. He answered the call and got up from his desk.

"Hey, babe! I...okay...shit." He headed toward the exit without a word to his partners. Grace and Isaac watched him go, concerned.

"What was that about?" Grace asked.

Isaac shook his head. "I don't know. First time I've seen David that concerned... probably ever." He glanced at his desk and all the paperwork, then looked at Grace's bigger pile of paperwork.

"You start your paperwork? It's how we get paid."

Grace looked at the mountain of paperwork on her desk; most of it was HR related.

"Uhh...." she stammered.

Isaac chuckled. He checked the clock on the wall and stood up.

"Come on, let's do that tomorrow. We got something more important to do."

Excitement pinged on Grace's face. "What is it?"

***

In the basement shooting range, Isaac and Grace approached their stall. Isaac set up a paper target of a human body and put it out to fifteen yards. Because of the time, the range was empty, which was a rare sight to behold.

"I saw the scores on your file. Your book work and street skills were exemplary, but your accuracy with a firearm-" Isaac trailed off.

Grace nodded sadly. "I've never been a great shot. I just can't seem to get the hang of it."

Isaac crossed his arms and looked Grace over.

"Bullshit," he declared. He pointed at her eyes. "You got eyes, correct?"

Grace nodded, a little amused.

He pointed at her hands. "You got fingers, correct?"

Grace nodded again.

Isaac pointed at the target. "Then you can be accurate with a firearm. Let's practice." He pulled out his Glock 21 from his holster. "They issue you your sidearm, yet?" he asked.

Grace shook her head. "No. They're doing that tomorrow. But I had a Glock 17 in Charleston."

Isaac nodded. He ejected the magazine from his Glock 21 and showed off the .45 ACP bullets.

"So, you were using 9mm, huh? It's faster and cheaper than the .45. I've thought about switching, but call me old school, I guess. They forced David to change his sidearm from a M1911 to a Glock, said he had to 'get with the times.'"

Grace chuckled. "Now that is old school," she joked.

Isaac handed her his Glock 21.

"Go ahead. Give me ten rounds on the target."

Grace "teacupped" the pistol and fired ten rounds rapidly. The slide locked back and Grace put down the pistol. Isaac pressed a button that made the target swing back to them. Grace's results weren't bad, but they weren't good either. Isaac picked up the pistol and handed it back to her.

"You're teacupping the pistol. They teach you that in Charleston?" he asked. Grace nodded.

Isaac raised his eyebrows.

"Now that is old school, and not good technique. Here, hold it like this." He positioned Grace's hands into a more-effective grip style with the non-dominant hand perched high and to the left of the dominant hand with both thumbs perfectly in line with each other.

"I'd show you by example but I'm currently using one hand, which isn't the most accurate way to fire," he muttered ruefully, touching his bandaged hand.

Grace frowned.

"I was going to ask about that injury."

Isaac shrugged.

"I punched a mirror," he said so nonchalantly, that Grace was speechless.

Isaac pointed at her grip. "That'll keep your aim steady and your purchase on the pistol more secure. Now, try again."

Grace loaded another ten bullets while Isaac sent the target out to fifteen yards. Grace emptied the magazine a little slower than the previous time. Isaac returned the target and looked over it.

"Not too bad. But there's still room for improvement." He sent the target out and started another drill for Grace to try.

***

It was 8 p.m. in the evening when they finished the drills. Isaac stuffed the dozen or so used targets into the recycle bin while Grace swept up the spent brass.

She looked over at Isaac.

"Was it too much to hope for an example from the teacher?" she asked. Isaac glanced again at his bandaged left hand, but Grace gave him an encouraging thumbs up. He shrugged.

"Well, we'll see." He attached a new target and sent it out to 25 yards. He loaded just five bullets into the pistol and grasped it with his good hand.

"Let's see." With one hand, Isaac fired all five rounds in rapid succession. The slide of the pistol locked back and Isaac placed it down on the rack. He flipped the switch and the target came back. Grace's jaw dropped at the results. Isaac rolled up the target and tossed it into the recycle bin without a word.

"I come down here almost every night," he stated.

Grace nodded, then took a deep breath.

"Do you mind if I ask you a personal question? It's not about your family."

"Go ahead."

"What's it like to kill someone?" she asked.

Isaac didn't answer at first. He stared down the length of the firing range and rubbed his eyes.

"It doesn't hit you at first. It's not until you're alone that you really feel it. How you react depends on what kind of person you are. The scariest thing is if you feel nothing."

Grace got back to sweeping brass. Isaac grabbed his empty Glock 21 from the stall shelf and holstered it. He turned to Grace. "You're a good kid, Grace. I wish you'd never come to Callahan."

Grace finished sweeping and the two moved to leave the firing range.

"I just hope I don't have to kill someone," she whispered.

Isaac sighed. "If you stay here long enough, you will."

***

The front door of the Murphy home swung open and Isaac stepped inside. He took one look at the utter disaster of his kitchen and dining room and turned away.

"Good job, Isaac." He dropped off his things and unholstered his firearm. He took it to the coffee table in the living room and placed it on the dark mahogany. Loosening his tie, he reached over to a cabinet and pulled out a black plastic case that held his gun cleaning kit. Cracking it open, he withdrew a few rags and some gun oil. He picked up the pistol, racked the slide back and ejected the loaded magazine along with the loose bullet. He then field stripped the pistol and got to work cleaning it. He took his time, since he only had one good hand. Methodically, he wiped down the pistol with the rag and a drop or two of solvent. Once finished cleaning, he squeezed a few drops of oil onto the slide rails and any other part that suffered from metal on metal friction. Isaac dropped one hollow point bullet back into the chamber and popped the slide forward. He slid in a loaded magazine and held the firearm in front of his face for inspection.

Isaac stared at the cold black steel of the firearm.

"Won't be enough," he muttered. He gingerly looked left. Clear. He looked right. Clear. He looked up. Clear. Isaac laid the pistol on the coffee table and stood up.

"Now for the mess." For the next hour Isaac cleaned up the wreckage, trashing anything that was broken and cleaning up all the stains and strewn food. He examined the dining room table and saw that it was damaged beyond repair. He pulled out big garbage bags and picked up all the pieces of broken mirror with his good hand. He carried the many garbage bags of rubble outside to the trash bin, and then rolled it to the street. He then awkwardly carried the dining room table out as well. It split in half at the halfway point, so he had to make two trips.

Back inside, he made a list of appliances and other replacements he would need to buy tomorrow. Casualties of his rage included a dozen drinking glasses, the microwave, the coffee pot, the dining table, the blender and the chef's knife he had cut himself with. Isaac glanced down at his hand, which was throbbing with pain. He flexed his fingers and cursed his destructive behavior.

Just as he finished the list, David called him. Isaac answered his phone.

"Hey, David, what time did you say? I know I'm late."

"Nope. We're still going strong. Bring some brews," his friend answered.

"Yuengling good?" Isaac asked, as he headed to his bedroom to change.

"For sure."

"I'll be there soon, then."

"Great! Bill's here by the way."

Isaac rolled his eyes. "Ah, Christ, that old fart?" he exclaimed.

David chuckled. "Man's wound up tighter than a drum. I figured it might help to relieve the stress a little."

Isaac shook his head and started to change into civilian clothes. He threw on a pair of jeans and an orange University of Miami t-shirt, his alma mater.

"Yeah alright. See ya in a bit, David."

"Later."

Isaac slipped the phone into his pocket and bent down to lace up some grey sneakers. He threw on a plain baseball cap and then headed into his closet to the safe. He withdrew a small inside-the-waistband holster with a compact Springfield 9mm pistol from his gun safe. He clipped the holster onto his belt and tucked the Springfield in between his jeans and underwear. He dropped the t-shirt over his beltline and the gun disappeared. While off-duty, Isaac couldn't open carry, so he concealed instead. He preferred it that way - No one would know he had a gun on him.

Before he flicked off the light, he stopped by the mirror next to the bed. He met the gaze of a man whose eyes shone with a seething fire. He could also see Emily's portrait, her face frozen in an eternal smile. He tore his gaze away from both and left the bedroom.

***

Isaac's car pulled into David's driveway. He parked it next to a half-dozen other cars, including David's motorcycle, before stepping out. He looked briefly at the passenger seat, where the freshly bought 12 pack of Yuengling sat. Isaac glanced down at his hand, which was still hurting. He'd changed the bandages again before leaving. He slowly closed his fist and winced at the jolt of pain.

"Isaac? That you? Hope you brought the beers because we're nearly out!" David called from the front porch.

Isaac gave a wave to David and then grabbed the twelve pack. He exited the car and started the walk to the porch. David lived in one of the many suburbs in Callahan County, but this far out from the city, the woods were in every direction. Isaac squinted at the dark tree line behind David's house. He thought he saw something moving in the shadows but blinked and it disappeared immediately. Perhaps it was just a shadow. He reached the stoop.

"Isaac! 'Bout time!" David exclaimed. His eyes were red and puffy. Isaac figured that he must have had plenty to drink.

"Damn! Already blitzed?" Isaac asked. David narrowed his eyebrows at Isaac, confused.

"No, I've only had a couple. I wanted to wait for you before I got into it."

Isaac had another look at David's bloodshot eyes, confused. He shook his head and waved it off.

"Oh, my mistake. Here," Isaac said as he stepped over the threshold and handed David the twelve pack. David gave him a playful tap on the shoulder.

"Come on! Everyone's waiting."

David and Isaac headed to the basement stairs. Along the way, Isaac noticed that neither Charlotte, nor David's daughter, Amy, seemed to be home. He held his tongue and didn't mention it. He didn't want to bring up something negative on a night that was supposed to be fun. He took a glance at David's nice southern home, perfect to raise a family in, before reaching the basement stairs.

Downstairs in the basement, the Texas hold 'em poker game was in full swing. David had the real deal too, an immaculate and professional poker table. He took the game quite seriously. Chief Laramie was indeed there, and a half-burnt cigarette dangled from his lips. He was sweating profusely and surprisingly drunk.

"Finally!" he called, "Here, toss me a beer!" Isaac threw him a beer and Laramie immediately popped it open and took a long swig. York was also there and had several empty bottles in front of him. He'd taken his glasses off and was very focused on the game. Next to him was Detective Johnson, a clean-cut, dark skinned, man in his mid-forties, and a good friend of David's. He adjusted his glasses and took a quick drag from a cigarette.

"Isaac, good to see you," he exclaimed.

Isaac shook the hand he offered.

"Same to you! Now who's going to deal me in?" Isaac took an empty seat and nodded at Officer Austin who was next him. Austin pulled out a metal tin of Snus smokeless tobacco and popped a pouch in between his cheek and gum before extending the tin towards Isaac.

"Isaac! Care for a pouch? It'll keep you focused," he said with a Beaufort twang.

Isaac shrugged and took a pouch, making Austin smirk. After sticking the pouch behind his upper lip, Isaac popped the tab on his beer and had a swig.

Laramie started dealing out the cards and the game resumed.

***

David, as usual, was winning by a longshot. He could probably go pro if his wife let him gamble for real money. Everyone was at various levels of intoxication, aside from Isaac, who was just nauseous. Austin had failed to tell Isaac how strong the nicotine in Snus was. Isaac spat it out after five minutes, but the damage had already been done. Meanwhile, Chief Laramie was four beers deep along with a considerable amount of honey whiskey. The bottle sat in front of him on the poker table's vibrant green felt, right next to his empty chip pile.

"Goddammit! David, I swear you cheatin! Every time I play you win!" Laramie slurred.

York chuckled, lighting up another cigarette as he beheld his own nonexistent chip pile.

"At least he didn't knock me out first this time! Thank Christ we don't play for money." He fished out another cigarette and handed it to Johnson, who happily accepted.

As York lit the cigarette, Johnson smiled through the smoke and said,

"I still consider myself a novice so it's okay that David shamed me right off the bat. Let's see if Isaac or Austin can pull off an upset." Austin popped two pouches into his mouth, which was going to make him absolutely wired. Isaac examined his hand. He had one king and two more were in the river, so this one should be in the bag. He raised and David immediately matched.

"Yeah, I got nothing," Austin muttered and folded. It was just Isaac and David now. David shot Isaac a death glare and Isaac did his best to match the intensity.

"Show 'em!" Laramie commanded.

Isaac put down his three of a kind. David put down a queen and the final king, giving him a full house. Isaac sighed. David grinned big and wide.

"Read 'em and weep, prettyboy!"

David's smile was almost too big, Isaac thought. It seemed like he was trying to convince everyone how happy he was.

David pulled his newly acquired chips in and rubbed his hands together. "This is gonna be it, you and Austin are on your last legs now."

Laramie dealt the new hand and Isaac picked up his cards. Without enough chips to pay for the blind, he and Austin would both have to go all in just to play the hand. Isaac glanced at his cards, nothing.

"Oh, boy," he muttered.

"Show 'em!" The three men flipped their cards. As expected, David won again, this time with three of a kind. Everyone at the table groaned, except for David.

"Woo! Bring me that money. King D wins again!"

Laramie stood up suddenly, spilling a little of the honey whiskey.

"Well, that's it for me. I'm gonna get some air."

David pouted. "What? Come on. How about we play for money this time? Don't tell your wife. I know you got a $20 in your pocket, Chief."

Laramie scowled. "First the $20, then the shirt off my back," he said. "Come on, let's go drink by the firepit. It's nice outside." Everyone but David agreed.

***

David had a classy stone firepit incorporated into his backyard, and all the men were camped around it, sitting on lawn chairs. Isaac tossed another log onto the fire and it roared up, nice and hot. He popped the tab on his third beer and took a nice swig. He had finally recovered from the potent nicotine high and made a mental note to never try chewing tobacco again.

A gentle breeze blew through the yard, causing the flames to flutter. The men had fallen quiet, just enjoying the cool spring breeze, the booze and the beautiful firelight.

Isaac leaned back in his chair and absentmindedly watched the tree line, now much closer than it was in the driveway.

"*There!*" Isaac jolted forward and rubbed his eyes. He was sure he saw something moving in the woods. He studied the trees, but the figure had disappeared once more.

"See something, Isaac?" David asked.

"I swear I just saw someone running in the trees, but I'm not sure."

David glanced over at the trees and shrugged.

"It's probably just a deer. The crackheads don't get this far out of the city," he joked. "If it is though, I'm pretty sure all of us are strapped right now."

Johnson narrowed his eyes.

"Maybe it's one of the Ghost Killers," he whispered melodramatically.

David chuckled and took a swig of beer. "Damn I wish it was. We could grab his ass and finally get some answers."

Isaac stared deep into the orange flames of the fire. The flickering lights reflected off his pale face and green eyes as he lost himself in the fire.

"Maybe it's the Wretched Man," he whispered. A cold shiver passed through the men; it was an icy flinch not even the hot fire could keep away.

Laramie scowled.

"Knock it off. I don't want to hear that damn name ever again!" he commanded.

York held up his hand to keep Laramie back.

"Hang on, Chief. Everyone listen up! I've got something to say about that," he said.

The men all looked at York curiously.

"What is it?" David asked.

York met eyes with Isaac and found the flames.

"I've thought about it and decided I want to change my rule on that. I don't agree with this 'refusing to utter the name' nonsense.

By avoiding the word like the plague, it just adds further negative connotation to it. It's a fairy tale. We shouldn't be so afraid of it. We shouldn't be afraid to say the name. Giving a name to a monster makes it less scary, real or not."

Some of the men nodded, but Laramie bared his teeth. "I don't want to utter the name of…. Well, *that name* because I want our focus to be on capturing real-life criminals, not ghosts."

"You're afraid of him. That's the real reason why you won't say his name," Isaac said.

The circle fell silent, with only the crackling of the fire making any noise. Laramie's face contorted and he started to argue. Suddenly, a gust of wind blew through the backyard. Johnson nervously checked left, right and up.

David squinted at him. "What was that?" he asked.

Johnson blushed a little, uncomfortable at being caught.

"Uh, I don't know. Just checking around me."

"Checking for what?" Laramie questioned, crossing his arms.

"The Wretched Man. It's how you check for him," Isaac answered. Johnson winced.

Laramie pursed his lips together, glowering at Isaac. "This is ridiculous!" he cried.

York shrugged. "Left. Right. Up. At least you can get a good visual of your surroundings that way."

Laramie smashed his honey whiskey bottle into the fire, causing the flames to soar into the sky. Everyone recoiled in surprise.

"Hey, now!" David exclaimed.

Laramie stood up and sneered at everyone. "I'm not going to sit here and listen to grown men, my own detectives, entertain the idea that a fairy tale is haunting this town! That thinking is turning this city into a madhouse, just one big echo chamber of fucking lunatics screaming at each other!"

"You still haven't said his name," Isaac pointed out.

Laramie poked a large finger in Isaac's face.

"I expect more from you, Detective Murphy. Emily would have been disgusted to see you entertain this bullshit."

Isaac lunged at Laramie, but David and York got between them.

"Settle down!" David yelled.

Isaac pulled away and sat back in his seat while Laramie dusted himself off and adjusted his askew glasses.

"Look, we got a little drunk, but that's no excuse for hurling comments like that, Chief. Why don't you apologize and then walk home to sleep it off?" David recommended.

Laramie sighed and extended his hand to Isaac.

"I'm sorry. That was uncalled for."

Isaac looked at Laramie's hand before shaking it.

"It's okay, Chief. It happens. I went too far as well." Isaac shook Laramie's hand.

Laramie turned to David and warned, "Y'all don't cause too much trouble now. We're still the law in this town." With that, Laramie left to trudge over to his house. He lived just up the road and didn't need to drive.

David checked his watch and saw that it was past 1 a.m. Another gust of wind blew in and he shivered.

"Sheesh. Y'all wanna head inside? It's starting to get blustery out here. And hey, if anyone wants to stay over, feel free."

Everyone started to head in, except Isaac, who continued to stare into the flames.

"Isaac?" David asked, questioningly.

"I'll be inside in a moment, just going to put out the fire," he answered.

David shrugged and followed the others. Isaac finished his last few swallows of beer and sat back in his chair. He closed his eyes and took a deep breath. "*Inhale. Count to five. Exhale. Count to five.*"

"Oh, Emily, what have I gotten myself into?" His words were whisked away into the wind. A drop of rain landed on his nose and he shivered.

"*Isaac....*"

Isaac's ears perked up and he looked to the right where the voice had come from. For a moment, he thought it must have been one of the guys, but then he remembered that they had all gone inside. He found himself staring at the tree line again. It was near pitch black past the glow of the fire, and the ominous black trees swayed in the wind just fifty feet away. Isaac squinted, trying to see through the darkness at where the voice came from.

"That wasn't the wind," Isaac whispered. He stood and took a few steps toward the tree line. He dug into his jacket and pulled out his phone. He clicked on the phone light and held it up, using the light to cut through the darkness, but it did very little to illuminate anything. He wished he'd brought his duty flashlight.

"Anyone there?" Isaac asked. He took another step and shined the pathetic phone light left and right but saw nothing. He shrugged and started to turn, but then he heard it. The unmistakable sound of crying. A man was weeping in the woods. Apprehensive, Isaac looked back at David's house, which now seemed very far away. He turned to the tree line, which was now just a few feet away.

"Dammit," Isaac swore. He reached his hand under his shirt and rested it on the cold steel of his compact Springfield. "Hello? Is anyone in there?" His words were swallowed by the darkness.

"*Help me, Isaac…* "

Isaac drew his pistol and snapped it up in front of him, training the glowing green night sights on the trees in front of him. He shivered and looked left. Clear. He looked right. Clear. He looked up. Clear. He took a bracing breath and entered the tree line.

"Police! Who's there?" he called out. He took a few more steps forward, and David's house disappeared. Isaac plunged deeper into the black woods, shining the phone flashlight, but seeing nothing.

"*I'm right here…* "

Isaac placed his finger on the trigger and aimed at a large tree in front of him. The voice was coming from behind it. Isaac shined his phone light around the corner and saw a pale hand lying on the ground, with the arm disappearing behind the tree. Isaac swallowed and began to pre-pull the trigger.

"Police. Don't move," he commanded in a shaking voice. He took a sidestep and pointed his gun behind the tree.

The Red Head's butchered corpse was filleted against the tree. His internal organs were strewn about the roots and two mangled eyes stared at Isaac from his shattered skull. Maggots crawled in and out of his busted eye sockets and feasted on the rotting intestines.

"Jesus Christ!" Isaac stumbled backward in shock. He tripped and his phone went flying from his bandaged hand. It was all he could do to not squeeze off a round as he fell onto his back. Isaac scrambled desperately for his phone, horrified at the pitch blackness surrounding him. He dug blindly at the dead leaves, trying to find his phone, which had landed facedown. At last he touched the case and with a cry of relief, raised both the light and his pistol at the tree.

The body was gone. No blood. No organs. Nothing. Just the rustle of leaves in the wind.

A cold sweat ran down Isaac's neck. His chest tightened and he felt like he couldn't breathe. He was sure something was on top of him. Slowly, with his muscles and bones creaking, he looked left. Clear. He looked right. Clear. Painfully, he looked up... clear. Isaac shakily got to his feet. He needed to get out of the woods, now. He took one last look at the tree where O'Donnell's body had been, then tore his gaze away.

"Emily, please protect me," Isaac whispered. He turned heel and sprinted from the woods, too terrified to look back. As he burst through the tree line, he nearly collided with David and York, and fell to the wet ground.

"Shit!" David yelped.

York helped Isaac to his feet as David looked on incredulously.

"What the hell were you doing in there? I thought you were just putting out the fire," York asked. "Why's your gun out?"

Isaac didn't know what to say. He holstered his pistol and then wiped his sweaty forehead.

"I... I had to see if anything was in there," he said in a low voice.

York peered into the woods and strained his neck for a better view but saw nothing. "Well, did you find something? Given your state, it looks like it."

Isaac tried to force a reassuring smile but failed.

"N...No. I just got spooked."

York and David exchanged a glance. They weren't buying it.

"Right…. Well, I think it's time we went home. Goodnight," York said, already walking to his car.

Isaac gave David a weary glower, who met it with a frown. The two returned to the house, where everyone else had already left. Isaac started to gather his things, but David stopped him with a pleading look.

"Would you, mind staying the night? Please? I'll make up the couch." David's voice broke on the final word.

Isaac was taken aback. He steeled himself and asked the question he'd been hoping to avoid.

"Where's Charlotte?"

"She told me she's not coming home tonight," David said blankly.

"Why?"

"She didn't say."

Isaac winced and asked the follow up question, "And Amy?"

"With Charlotte."

Isaac felt the pain of that flat statement like a knife in his sternum. He gave his best friend a hug. They held it for a moment and David blinked back tears.

"It's going to be all right, big guy, I'll stay tonight. Okay? Neither one of us should be alone right now," Isaac promised. David walked into the kitchen and poured another drink.

"I hope so, buddy. I really do." David knocked back another shot.

BOBBIT ROCK

4. The Boiling Point

"It's about to turn into the Wild West out here."

David shook Isaac awake a few hours later.

"Hey, wake up. Charlotte just pulled in with Amy. Try to look like you're not hungover."

"Well, shit," Isaac groaned. He sat up on the couch and the pang of a headache smacked him between his eyes.

"Shit. How many shots did we have?" Isaac asked.

David cocked his head at Isaac.

"What shots?" he asked.

Isaac rubbed his temples. "Ah, Christ," he moaned.

David handed Isaac a mug of hot coffee and he gulped it down thankfully. David lifted Isaac to his feet and Isaac shakily found his balance. David never had hangovers, while Isaac always felt like he'd been hit by a truck.

The front door opened, and Isaac pasted on a fake smile. Charlotte stopped in the threshold and looked at the two men. Her hair was pulled up in a tight bun and her mouth was creased with lines from years of smoking, just like David's.

"Hey, babe! Good morning," David said cheerily.

Charlotte barely looked at him, but gave him a quick, emotionless, kiss as she stepped inside. Clutching her left hand, was little Amy, who rushed forward and hugged Isaac. She barely reached his waistline.

"Uncle Isaac!" she squealed.

Isaac tussled her messy blond hair, the same color as David's.

"Hey, kid, have a good trip?" he asked. Amy smiled wide, her merry brown eyes shining, and showed off the empty spot where a baby tooth had been.

"Uh, huh! We went to Charleston! And one of my teeth fell out, look!"

This happy child was one of Isaac's favorite people on earth. The two couples had been so close that Emily and Isaac were set to be Amy's legal guardians in case a tragedy happened, and vice versa for Samantha.

Isaac smiled and examined her mouth.

"Wow! Amy!" He held up a high five and Amy smacked it. David turned to Charlotte.

"We should talk," he suggested. Charlotte pushed past him, towards the kitchen.

"Later. I have to head to the office. You're off today, correct? Can you watch her?"

David's shoulders slumped and he looked down at his feet, defeated.

"Yes. Of course."

Charlotte grabbed a pre-made smoothie from the refrigerator and headed back to the door. She stopped and gave Isaac a small, but sincere, smile.

"Always good to see you, Isaac. How have you been feeling?" she asked.

"One day at a time," he stated dully.

Charlotte nodded. "David and I are here for you," she added as she closed the door behind her.

Amy rushed to David and he lifted her up for a big hug. For a moment, David was the happiest man in the world. Isaac couldn't help but grin at the sweet scene.

"Daddy! Did you see my tooth? Did you see my tooth?!" Amy exclaimed.

David laughed and set her down.

"What tooth? There's just a big hole! You're a big girl now! Who knows, maybe next week you'll be taller than me." Amy's eyes grew wide.

"Woah!" she exclaimed in wonder.

Isaac couldn't help but to crack up. David patted her on the head.

"Now why don't you play some games on the television while Uncle Isaac and I talk. Hmmm?"

Amy ran off to the television and booted up the family Play-Station. David motioned for the porch and the two men walked outside. Outside, David kept the porch door cracked so he could keep an ear and eye on Amy. He pulled out a cigarette and lit it up. He offered Isaac one. Isaac obliged. For a moment the two shared a quiet moment. David finished his cigarette and ashed it out. Isaac did the same, but he'd only smoked about half of it. Isaac sighed and looked at the tree line.

"You know we used to talk about her so much, Emily and I. God, Emily would go on and on about how much she loved Amy," Isaac said.

David smiled softly.

"I love her too. She really is just amazing. You're so lucky to be raising such a wonderful girl," Isaac added.

David gave Isaac a pat on the back and spoke, "It was Amy's idea to call you two aunt and uncle, and it's because she loved you two that much. I'm glad we set up that legal guardianship. Even though… things changed, I can think of no one better than you to watch over her."

Isaac glanced back at Amy, who was engrossed in the videogame.

"You're a survivor, Isaac. You always have been, even since back when we were kids. You've got someone watching over you."

Isaac's eyelid twitched. *"Someone on my shoulders."*

"Things are not good. This city is falling apart. Charlotte and I… I'm just glad to know that Amy will always have someone to look after her… someone I can trust," David continued.

Isaac couldn't find any words to say. An image flashed in his mind, him holding baby Samantha in his arms….

Isaac's fingers gripped the wood railing of the porch tightly. His knuckles turned white. For a brief second, he stood hard as a rock, every muscle taut. The tension released.

"You can trust me. I'll always have your back." He turned to David and gave him a reassuring smile. "But it won't be necessary. Everything will be fine." Isaac's words felt hollow.

***

Isaac's head was still filled with his wife and little girl as he drove home. It started to rain as he stared with glassy eyes at the road in front of him. Traffic was very light on a Sunday morning this far out from the city. Isaac soon found himself alone on the two-lane road. Isaac glanced over at the empty seat next to him, the one that she used to sit in. Although it was her car, he often drove when they were together.

"*Isaac...*"

Isaac turned his gaze again to the passenger seat, where the voice had come from. "Emily?" he whispered. The seat was empty and Isaac was alone. He shook his head and returned his gaze to the road.

"Fuck!" he screamed.

Isaac saw the pedestrian, but it was far too late to stop. He blew through the red light and hit the man at 50 mph. The man smashed face first into the windshield, cracking and splattering the windshield with blood, before flipping over the roof and crumpling onto the asphalt behind the car. The tires squealed as Isaac slammed the brakes and the car fishtailed, before skidding to a halt in the pouring rain. Isaac kicked open the door and bolted from the car toward the body.

"Oh, Christ," he stammered as he approached the mangled corpse. "I'm so sorry. Sir, can you hear me? Can you-" Isaac froze when he saw the man's face. It was the Red Head. His body looked exactly like how it did at the crime scene and in the woods, butchered. His severed cheek was on full display as well.

Isaac took a slow deep breath and closed his eyes. When he opened them, the body was gone. His knees buckled and he sat down heavily. He put his face in his hands and shook uncontrollably as the rain chilled him to the bone.

"Please make it stop. Please, God make it stop," he begged. The sound of an approaching car made him look up. A grey sedan pulled next to him and a middle-aged woman rolled down the passenger window.

"You okay, honey? Car trouble?" she asked.

Isaac looked at her and the concerned face of her husband. He mustered up enough energy to choke out the words, "I'm... fine."

The woman glanced over at her husband. He jerked his head towards the road, and she sighed.

"Be safe, then!" she said as the husband hit the gas.

Isaac slowly rose to his feet. He squished back to his car before falling into the driver's seat and shutting the door. He looked in sick wonder at the undamaged windshield. Just moments ago, it had been cracked and covered in blood and brain matter. Now there was nothing. Isaac touched the windshield and traced a finger down the glass.

"Am I losing my mind?" he asked. The only response was the pattering rain. Isaac steadied his breath and reached for the gearshift. That's when he felt it... his shoulder was numb. The numbness quickly extended down his arm and into his fingers until he felt only pins and needles. They took over his left arm just as quick. He didn't realize that he'd stopped breathing. A scream began to build deep inside his chest, but it wasn't going to come out. He was trapped in a massive panic attack.

Isaac instinctively reached for his head but couldn't lift his arms. His chest was burning, and he hadn't figured out why. He heard a rushing in his ears and felt lightheaded. The corners of his vision darkened, and an inverted black circle began to constrict his vision. "*Breathe!*"

Isaac managed a gasp and immediately started hyperventilating. The breath stopped his chest from burning, but the hyperventilating made the cabin start spinning.

"Please God! Make it stop!" Isaac tried to grip the steering wheel for support as the interior of the car started spinning, but his arms were like blocks of lead. He turned his gaze to the roof of the car and helplessly pleaded, "Emily! Please don't leave me! I'll do anything!" With the walls of his vision closing in, he pushed his shoulder into the door and almost fell onto the wet asphalt.

Free from his claustrophobia, Isaac heaved himself against the back of the car and labored through the panic attack. "*Inhale. Count to five. Exhale. Count to five.*"

He managed to control his breathing and slowly felt feeling return to his arms. The shaking continued, and Isaac realized it wasn't going to stop anytime soon. He crawled back into the driver's seat, now completely drenched by the cold rain and the runoff from his soaked clothes. Isaac fumbled with the gearshift before finally taking off onto the road. Five minutes later he arrived home amid another panic attack. He stumbled out of the car and pushed his way inside before collapsing onto the living room sofa. He closed his eyes and immediately lost consciousness.

***

Three hours later, Isaac languished under the spray of hot water from the shower. He grasped the shower head and inhaled the hot steam. His heart was still beating quickly from the two panic attacks he'd suffered.

Once he felt a little better, he left the shower and sat, wrapped in blankets, in a recliner. The television in front of him flashed with the afternoon Callahan news... more murders, more madness. Isaac took a bite from a microwave burrito and tried to breathe as slowly as possible as the horrors of the morning were recounted by an emotionless female anchor.

Around 7 p.m., Isaac shut off the television and moved to his bedroom. He crawled underneath the covers and grabbed the portrait of Emily, holding it close to his chest before pulling the covers up to his chin and shutting his eyes tight.

"I love you, my dear," he whispered.

**

Dawn had not yet broken when Isaac woke up and wandered into his home office. In the center of the room, splayed out on the carpet was a large mess of folders, pictures and files. It was Emily's case. Isaac walked past it wordlessly. He sat down at the old wooden desk, an antique that belonged to his grandmother, and clicked on the lamp.

There were boxes and boxes of manila case folders against the walls that held information on every case he had ever investigated. A professional scanner he used to turn every paper into a digital file was also within arm's reach. On the desk was also a large hard drive that served as his backup.

He booted up the computer and reached into the closest box, withdrawing the O'Donnell file. The folder was noticeably thin. He flipped it open and sighed, unsure of what he was hoping to accomplish. He thumbed through the useless forensics details and briefly stared at the photo of O'Donnell's corpse. The injuries were identical to those he'd seen in his two… hallucinations? Isaac shuddered and closed the file. He rubbed his eyes and rested his forehead on the mahogany desktop, breathing slowly.

A thought came to him, so he lifted his head and walked over to Emily's case. There was much more to look at with this case, since Isaac had clearly poured over every aspect of it with excruciating detail. Unfortunately, his frustration was also apparent in the mess of strewn papers, scrawled comments and coffee stains. He sat down on the floor and looked over the disaster he had left last time. Carefully, he started to organize everything. A hospital photo of a deceased Emily fell from a stack while he was organizing, and Isaac couldn't pull his gaze from the love of his life, torn up and brutalized by the stab wounds. Her ear had been sliced off and there was a vicious gash in her cheek. A large horizontal slice spanned her belly from the emergency C-Section. He shoved the photo back into the stack with a trembling hand and continued cleaning up.

When he had coordinated everything, he withdrew the list of evidence for the deceased. He skimmed through the notes he'd read a thousand times and moved on to photos of the crime scene. There was blood spatter in the dining room from where Emily was first attacked. The blood trail went up the stairs as she tried to reach the guns in the bedroom. The lower walls were splayed with blood halfway up from the severed artery in her leg. Isaac skipped over the dozens of photos of Emily, unable to stomach the sight anymore. He glanced over the photos of shell casings, his, and the bullet hole in the wall. He finally studied the photos of the shattered living room window and accompanying blood stains. "*So damn close....*"

Past that shattered window, the Bobbit Rock loomed in the woods.

The pinky and ring finger of the suspect had been recovered from the scene. Isaac stared at the photo of the severed appendages with grim satisfaction. There were no matches for the fingerprints, of course. No matching DNA either. The suspect was either a first time criminal, a mastermind or a ghost. Finally came the police sketch. Isaac bored his eyes into the man who killed his wife and unborn daughter. For a moment, he was sure the sketch would burst into flames from the burning rage he cast upon it. But it didn't, the killer just stared back, unblinking. Nobody outside close friends even seemed to care about Emily's death. In murder town, who cared if a pregnant woman got stabbed in her own home? It made 15 seconds on the nightly news, which had to make room for the other murders that day.

"I am going to find you. You son of a *bitch!*" Isaac vowed.

But there were no leads. The perp's modus operandi was identical to many of the murders that happened in Callahan, with no substantial evidence, no leads and thus no case. If the Ghost Killers were real, perhaps this man was one of them.

Isaac got to his feet and left the office, slamming the door in frustration. He went to his gun safe and withdrew the Glock 21. He then went downstairs to the dining room. He raised the pistol and aimed it at the stairs. He imagined the moment when the killer stabbed Emily in the thigh. If only his aim had been better. He'd spent the last three months obsessively in the firing range, rectifying that mistake. It made no difference to Emily now. He glanced at the bullet hole in the wall and remembered the pain in the killer's eyes when the fingers were shot off.

Isaac trained the sights on the front door and his finger touched the trigger.

"If I'd already been home…." Isaac started to squeeze the trigger at the door, imagining that dark figure pushing through the threshold, only to catch a .45 ACP in his mouth.

Isaac sat on the floor and looked at the Glock 21. It was austere. It was ugly. It was death. *"Why couldn't it kill that motherfucker?"*

Isaac was gripping the pistol so hard that his fingers were starting to ache. He began to pull the trigger. He could see the killer's eyes from above the bandana, looking in shock at his mangled hand. Isaac opened his eyes and took his finger off the trigger, coming back to earth with no time to spare. He locked the slide back, which sent the live bullet clattering to the floor. He ejected the magazine and methodically field stripped the pistol. He stared at the pieces of the pistol with a fire burning in his eyes and grief filling his heart.

***

A week later, Isaac awoke on a quiet Sunday morning and considered going to church; Emily would have wanted to go. They used to go every Sunday, but since her death, Isaac couldn't stand it. Churchgoers had supported him initially after her death, but the whole place was falling into nihilistic despair as more parishioners, relatives and friends turned up dead.

"I wish we'd left this city, Emily," Isaac whispered to the ever-present portrait. Isaac put the portrait aside on the bed and sat up. It was 9 a.m. and he was hungry. He moved to the bathroom and brushed his teeth. He glanced at the unshaven stubble on his face and shrugged. In the kitchen he opened the fridge and decided to make something nice. A short while later, he was munching on a tasty mushroom omelet with a side of fruit and a steaming hot mug of green tea. He'd even made a little fire in the fireplace to ward off the unusual morning chill. He absentmindedly flipped through a newspaper, trying to avoid all the articles about murder and death. The front page featured a photo of a woman crying next to a covered stretcher with the headline "When will the Murders End?" An editorial article was titled "Fire the Chief of Police." Another showed a ghastly charcoal drawing of the Wretched Man with the label "What is the Wretched Man?" Isaac glanced at the charcoal sketch of the Wretched Man; it wasn't very accurate to what he had seen in his past. The drawing was world renowned and had been sketched in the mid-1800's. The face was obscured in shadow. No one had ever seen his face, except for Isaac and Bobbit.

Isaac tore out the charcoal drawing and placed it on the replacement dining table. He pushed away from the table and walked over to the living room. After rummaging through a cabinet, he came back with Emily's sketch book and a pencil. He closed his eyes and thought about that night as a child, when the Wretched Man latched onto him. He opened his eyes and began drawing the nightmarish face.

He started with the eyes, or what could be considered eyes, those hollow, mangled, sockets. The air chilled as Isaac sketched the face of the devil. He drew the mouth, a gaping maw. Then he drew the leathery skin that was torn by time.

Rot and stench seemed to permeate off the paper and the air began to reek of sulfur. The monster came alive on the paper and Isaac sketched furiously, unable to stop. His shoulders tightened as his hand took on a twisted life of its own. A piercing scream filled Isaac's ears and his vision narrowed.

"Stop!" he gasped. He flung the pencil away and took a deep breath. Isaac wiped the sweat from his eyes and stared at the paper in terror. His heart skipped a beat and he exhaled.

"Thank God. I didn't finish it," he choked. The sketch was only half complete, only the eyes and mouth had been drawn. Isaac backed away from the sketch, trying to escape the hateful aura that was pouring out from that face. He ran to the kitchen and grabbed a lighter. He clutched the sketch over the sink and held it to the flame. Nothing happened. Isaac stared incredulously at the unmarred sketch. The Wretched Man stared back.

Isaac grabbed the paper with both hands and tried to rip it to shreds, but he may as well have been tearing at solid steel.

"Jesus Christ," Isaac gasped. The paper shivered in his hand.

The fireplace flickered out of the corner of his eye and without hesitation, Isaac tossed the sketch onto the flames. He turned and refused to look at the results. He stumbled back to his breakfast and sat down heavily, putting his face in his hands.

"Did that just happen?" he whispered. He took a breath and tried to get back to his breakfast. He shoved down the now cold eggs and swallowed the rest of the fruit. That's when he heard it. His cellphone was ringing upstairs. The phone went to voicemail. Immediately the caller dialed again, and it rung again.

"Jeez," Isaac muttered. He reached his bedroom and pulled his phone off the charger. It was David. Isaac raised the phone to his ear.

"David?" he asked. On the other end, David was driving his squad car. He was in full gear and had a rifle in the passenger seat next to him.

"Isaac! What the hell! Where are you?" he demanded. Isaac recoiled from his emotional tone.

"I'm at home. What's wrong?" he asked.

David wiped a sheen of sweat from his brow. "Jesus man, don't you watch the news? The hospital just got bombed! Lots of casualties."

"Okay…" Isaac stammered.

David swore loudly. "Get suited up and get your ass to the hospital ASAP."

Isaac glanced at his car, remembering what happened a few nights before. He gritted his teeth.

"Can you give me a ride?" he asked painfully.

David raised his eyebrows but then nodded. "Sure, whatever. It's on the way. Five minutes. Gear up because we don't know what we're going into. And get your head on straight!"

David hung up and Isaac stared at his phone in a dazed silence.

***

David and Isaac sped through the streets towards the hospital. As they drove, other squad cars with sirens screaming joined them. A fire engine sped by as well.

"That firetruck is from the next county over; all hands-on deck," David muttered.

The radio was going crazy with reports and chatter from ground zero. York's voice finally boomed, "Hospital has not been cleared yet. Attending officers should wait for the bomb squad and SWAT team to go through. Wait until the All Clear is given. All medical personnel are to wait until the All Clear is given. Repeat, hospital is not clear." In the background, the anguished cries of the wounded could be heard.

"Jesus, look at that," Isaac said, pointing at a large plume of black smoke that was rising into the sky. David gulped and made the last turn. Isaac racked the charging handle of an AR–15 as David hit the brakes.

"Here we go," Isaac breathed.

David killed the engine and the two jumped out with their rifles.

It was pandemonium. First responders from every department were running around in a panic trying to perform a dozen different duties. The press had swamped the perimeter, along with dozens of civilians, desperate to hear about the status of their loved ones. Wounded were everywhere, and they were just the ones who'd been able to walk out. EMTs were already triaging the injured and bundling them onto stretchers toward awaiting ambulances.

"Gonna have to send them to every hospital within a hundred-mile radius," David said. "A lot of people are gonna die en route..." he added morosely.

Two EMTs barreled through the crowd, nearly knocking Isaac over. He gaped at the wounded woman on the gurney they were rolling. One of her legs had been blown off at the hip; the other was riddled with shrapnel. She met Isaac's gaze as she was carried by, and the agony in her eyes ripped through Isaac's heart.

"Isaac! Come on!" David snapped.

Isaac wrenched his gaze away from the woman and pushed forward toward the edge of the perimeter. He was finally able to get a good look at the hospital. The fire department had just finished putting out the last of the flames. Captain York, who was standing at the edge of the perimeter, got a call on his radio.

"Fire is out, but there is significant structural damage to the ICU. The rest of the hospital should be clear to enter," the Fire Chief said. York nodded and issued a command into his radio.

"SWAT team and bomb squad, you are clear to enter!" The teams pushed forward into the hospital.

David and Isaac approached York.

"Are there active hostiles in the hospital?" David asked.

York glanced at him with a thousand-yard stare. He was shell-shocked and running on pure adrenaline. "Doesn't look like it. Just the bombs. SWAT team is a precaution."

York's radio crackled.

"Captain York! Every second we aren't in there more people are dying. How much longer before medical can go in?!" a doctor roared at York. York raised the radio to his mouth.

"Wait for the All Clear. We have to wait for it to be safe," York answered.

"There is no safe," a nearby EMT snapped.

York put the radio down and rubbed his temples.

"Where's Chief Laramie?" Isaac asked.

"I don't know. Haven't been able to reach him. No one has seen him since the call first went out."

Another gurney was wheeled by and they looked at the wounded man. His chest had been slashed open in a very familiar way. An EMT gave Isaac a quick shake of the head as they passed. The message was clear: The man was done for.

"That doesn't look like shrapnel," David stated dryly.

York swore loudly. Isaac spoke up, "So, the Ghost Killers blow up the hospital and then stab the survivors? If so, where are they? They'd still be in there…"

"If that was the case, we'd be hearing gunshots right now from SWAT," York stated. "No, they escaped amidst the chaos."

"Well, we've got to have them on camera this time for sure, not to mention all the witnesses."

York held up a hand to silence David's hopes. "No, we'll be lucky to get anything. The first report was that the power got cut to the hospital, backup generators too. Then five minutes later it blows up. But I already put the order out to close the points of exit to the city. Everyone is getting searched," York stated dryly.

Isaac smacked his hands together angrily. "That's not good enough! They just blew up a hospital! We are going to find evidence this time, there's no way in hell we won't."

York didn't reply. A moment later, his radio crackled.

"Building's clear. No hostiles. No more explosives. But it's a bloodbath in here. Send 'em in."

York nodded and raised the radio to his lips.

"All Clear. First responders go in first. May God help us."

***

As the first responders rushed in, Isaac and the rest of the detectives waited for their call to enter. David continued to grill York.

"How could the Ghost Killers have pulled this off? How were the bombs placed? Did we not have officers stationed here to protect against this very thing?" David peppered the questions at York who had had just about enough.

"David. I'm sorry, but I can't answer all this. We're still trying to figure things out. Excuse me, but I have to manage this." York got back on his radio as others immediately jumped on him demanding more answers. A female journalist shoved a microphone into his face, spouting questions, until an officer pushed her away.

"Isaac! David!"

The two detectives turned to see Grace. Her uniform was ruffled up and she was wired with stress.

"Grace? Any chance you have some answers?" Isaac asked.

Grace frowned.

"Perhaps. I was one of the first who got here. The rumor is that two bombs went off. But as you've probably seen, people are showing trauma not caused by explosions, burns or shrapnel."

A line of doctors and surgeons met the wounded as they were taken into ambulances, some emergency operations were being performed in the parking lot. Grace watched with visible distress. "The disconcerting thing is that some of the wounded have been talking about the Wretched Man," she muttered.

David spat on the ground. "Figures."

Isaac leaned forward. "What have they been saying?" he asked.

Grace sighed. "God knows. Just before y'all got here, I saw a woman howling that the Wretched Man had risen the dead. Then they started cutting people up with 'claws.'"

Isaac's mouth twitched at that word, but he was interrupted by a voice calling out,

"It's Chief Laramie!" Everyone turned to see the Chief slowly plod his way through the crowd. His eyes stayed glued to his feet as he made the march to the edge of the perimeter where they stood. He stopped in front of York.

"Bill?" York asked.

Laramie met York's gaze. The look of absolute defeat on Laramie's face was overwhelming. He reached to his shirt and pulled off his badge. He handed the badge to York, who took it, stunned.

"I'm sorry, Anthony. It's in your hands now." Without another word, and never even looking at the hospital, Bill Laramie turned his back on his department and left Callahan forever. Detectives and officers looked on, some with tears in their eyes as the defeated Laramie walked to his car and drove away.

York stared at Laramie's badge for a long time. He took in a slow breath, cleared his throat and tucked the badge into his pocket. He lifted his gaze to the men and women he now commanded.

"Detectives are clear to enter. Let's go."

Everyone pushed into the hospital. There was still a haze of smoke inside and Isaac coughed as he entered. They pushed through the haze and took in the scene. It was an absolute blood bath, with dead and wounded everywhere. Many victims were missing body parts. An elderly patient shuffled past Isaac. His whole face was drenched in blood as EMTs carefully led him out. Isaac stopped in front of a pile of bodies.

"There's someone alive in there!" an officer called out.

Isaac and the officer rushed forward and grabbed the twitching hand sticking from the pile. They pulled out a catatonic woman and handed her to the EMTs. She collapsed in their arms.

Isaac moved through the massacre in a daze, doing what he could to help the wounded. At some point, he ran into Grace amidst the madness. She had on latex gloves and they were bright crimson from the blood of countless victims. She was helping a pair of EMTs deal with a young nurse who had several large lacerations on her torso. Isaac noted that the wounds were fatal. These were her final moments.

"Skin like leather. Pale as ash. The Wretched Man," she gasped as blood bubbled through her lips. Her eyes darted left and right in horror, terrified of what she might see.

Isaac's ears perked up from her words and he took a step forward. "What did you see?" he asked.

The woman turned her gaze to Isaac and her eyes widened, fixed on a point directly above Isaac's head. Pure terror erupted in her eyes and she screamed literal bloody murder at Isaac. Everyone followed her gaze but only saw the empty air above Isaac's head. She started to choke on the blood. The EMTs prepared to intubate her, but it was too late. Grace took Isaac's hand and led him away as she died.

"Come on. There are others we can help," Grace said.

Isaac said nothing, unable to forget the echo of the woman's scream or the terror in her eyes as she looked above him. He cast his gaze left. Clear. Right. Clear. Up. Clear. He saw nothing, and yet, he knew he was being watched. The Wretched Man was here.

"Where's David?" Isaac choked out.

Grace motioned toward a long hallway. "I think I saw him head towards the loading bay."

Isaac started off but Grace grabbed his hand with consternation in her eyes.

"Isaac. I know something is wrong, more than this horror today. Please, if you ever need someone to talk to about anything, I'm here," she promised.

Isaac nodded his appreciation.

"Thank you, Grace."

He turned and pushed through the door to the loading bay. He stopped dead in his tracks at the gory spectacle. "Jesus Christ."

The loading bay was heavily damaged from the bombs and puddles of blood dotted the site from where bodies had been. The EMTs had nearly finished with the last of the victims. However, there was one body they hadn't been able to reach.

Hanging upside-down from the ceiling by her foot, was a young woman. She was Japanese, and a vicious slice across her abdomen had caused a torrent of blood to run down her face and hair and form a large pool beneath her. Even now, a steady drip of blood fell fifteen feet from her hair to the floor. Isaac couldn't even look at her - it was pure nightmare inducing terror. Her expression was frozen in agony and her blood-filled eyes stared forward.

David was staring at the upside-down woman in stunned silence, mouth agape. Other officers and paramedics did the same.

"How did she even get up there?" an EMT whispered.

Isaac approached David, who hadn't noticed his arrival.

"David?" he asked.

David didn't respond. He was a million miles away.

Isaac gave him a bit of a shove on the shoulder. "David! Snap out of it."

David broke from his trance and looked at Isaac.

"Isaac? Shit. Thank God you're here," he stammered.

"I was just with you when we went in, remember?"

David shook his head. "Right. Sorry. Shit." David turned to the others.

"Stop gawking! One of you find a ladder and bring her down!" he demanded harshly.

The officers tore their gaze away from the woman and scrambled to find a ladder.

Isaac wrung his hands through his hair. "Is this really happening?" he asked.

"Yes." David breathed, checking his watch, "Almost time," he added. "The Feds are taking over. The mayor is giving a press conference at noon. There's some National Guard general here, too. There's a bigwig doctor from the medical university who's supposed to talk as well. Today was the straw that broke the camel's back."

One of the wounded who was being tended to by an EMT suddenly cried out violently, "The Wretched Man! I saw him! He's here! He'll take your skin!" he wailed.

Isaac grimaced. "I hope that doctor can explain the-"

"The fact that people are claiming they've seen the Wretched Man?" David finished.

The EMTs carried out the hysterical man. He screamed the whole way. "He's coming! He's coming back for me! He'll take my eyes! Please help me!" An EMT looked at Isaac helplessly. Isaac watched him go, stone-faced.

David threw his hands up. "Laramie's gone and York's a mess. The hospital is blown up. The best doctors in Callahan are dead or dying. Old folks are dead. Pregnant women are dead. Babies... dead... This can't be happening."

Isaac clapped David on the back.

"This is more than anyone signed up for," he said.

"We don't even know if the Ghost Killers are real," David said.

"But a lot of people believe the Wretched Man is," Isaac responded.

David rubbed his face with his hands. "The Ghost Killers have to be real," he pleaded.

Isaac nodded and then spoke.

"If they aren't real...."

The officers returned with a rickety ladder and set it up under the upside-down woman and began to pull her down.

"Be careful," Isaac warned.

David motioned at the wreckage and blood around them. "There has to be evidence from this. We have to find something. Anything. We may not have camera footage, but fingerprints, blood work, something," David sighed.

Isaac shrugged. "Maybe. Maybe even from the remains of the bombs. Perhaps we can make a connection. If it was fertilizer based, maybe we could look up recent sales?"

One of the officers reached out with gloved hands and gingerly got ahold of the upside-down woman's head.

"National Guard and the Feds, huh? Are we getting canned?" Isaac asked.

David chuckled coldly. "No, they're gonna need all the help they can get." David gave Isaac an intense stare. "It's about to turn into the Wild West out here. Every news company will be here 24/7. People will travel from all over just to see the 'cursed city of Callahan.' We'll all be under the microscope and the Feds will be looking for scapegoats. Watch your ass, Isaac. The world will be watching Callahan, South Carolina," David declared.

"I guess our little hellhole couldn't stay hidden forever. I wonder if they'll impose martial law?" Isaac asked.

David shook his head. "No way. That'd be the end. It can't happen."

Isaac pointed at the upside-down woman.

"How did she get up there? Anything's possible now."

David crossed his arms. "So, what, we're gonna get grilled by Suits about whether or not we're traitors? Whether we're the Ghost Killers? This is bullshit."

"Just try not to get shot on your way home by a soldier who thinks you're a Ghost Killer," Isaac said dryly.

David's face darkened and he turned from Isaac and moved toward the corner of the loading bay. Isaac watched him go, perplexed. Suddenly, a small whimper escaped David's lips.

"David?" Isaac asked, concerned.

David faced forward, not wanting Isaac to see his watery eyes. He took a slow breath and let it out. "Charlotte's divorcing me."

Isaac flinched and rubbed a hand over his face.

"I'm sorry," he said softly. "Here, let's find some place private," he added. He took David by the arm and they found a little technician room for privacy. As soon as the door shut, David began to crumble.

"I was hoping we could work it out. I knew she was cheating on me. Turns out, she's been having an affair with some bigshot lawyer in Charleston. Her divorce lawyer showed up to the house the other day and served me the papers. I had to sign," David whispered.

Isaac closed his eyes. "How bad?" he asked, afraid of what he would hear.

David withdrew a cigarette. He stuck it into his lips and tried to light it, but his hands were shaking too much. Isaac lit it for him. "Well it ain't good. She doesn't care about the house because her boyfriend has a mansion on Shem Creek. No, she just wants Amy. And she'll get her, full custody for sure."

Isaac felt his blood boil.

"Bullshit. She can't get full custody."

A smile crossed David's face, the grin of a man about to be executed, who knows all he can do is laugh at the unfortunate hand he's been dealt.

"They've spun up the accusations. They'll go before the court and Charlotte will say I was a raging alcoholic who beat her regularly. I'm sure they'll doctor up some photos of her with a bruised face, too. Amy's too young to understand, so she'll say whatever Charlotte tells her to." David took a long drag off his cigarette.

"They also served me a restraining order this morning, just to add fuel to the fire. So, I can't even see Amy. Remember, Charlotte's fucking a bigshot lawyer; he'll know exactly how to game the system. In short, I'm screwed."

"You have to fight!"

David shrugged Isaac off.

"It doesn't matter what's true in divorce court. She's got the lawyers and the court is on her side. It's over. Whatever she says will become fact... I'm going to lose Amy-" David burst into tears and Isaac tried his best to reassure him.

"Come on man. We'll get through this. We'll get-"

David coughed and wiped his eyes, regaining his composure. "I'm okay. I'm okay, can't let it, affect my job." David cleared his throat and took a breath. He squared his shoulders and left the technician room with Isaac following.

Back in the loading baby, David looked up as the officers finally lowered the woman's body. They laid her onto a stretcher and the EMTs prepped her to be moved.

As she lay there, her unmoving eyes fixed on David's, trapping him in her gaze. He tore his gaze away and looked up at the ceiling for escape. A flash of panic crossed his face. He stared back at the corpse on the ground, then at the ceiling. He did this several times, until Isaac noticed his darting irises.

"Hey, stop looking at her. It's just another corpse. We've seen countless."

David turned to Isaac, and Isaac was repulsed by the sickness in his gaze.

"Not this one," David said ominously. David looked to his left. Clear. He looked to his right. Clear. He looked up. Clear.

***

The press conference was about to begin. All the major news corporations were there with camera's rolling, Meanwhile, outside town hall, hundreds of people were protesting. The National Guard, in full riot gear, was holding them back. Amidst the crowd, a man held aloft a giant paper mâché figure of the Wretched Man in all his vile glory. His face was covered, as always. Around the figure, a group of protestors held up signs reading "The Wretched Man Is Here."

Isaac and Grace watched the conference on a television in a hospital waiting room. David, completely inconsolable, lingered behind them, trying to keep himself together. Isaac put a reassuring hand on David's shoulder before turning his attention to the screen.

Inside town hall, Mayor Langston Bailey, the epitome of a southern gentleman, approached the podium to the tune of a hundred snapping cameras. Bailey looked like a dead man. He was sweaty and pale green, a man trying hard not to vomit in front of an audience of millions. His aide flicked on a microphone and spoke into it quickly.

"Please observe a moment of silence for the lives lost today."

The room quieted and Bailey bowed his head. When the moment ended, he stepped up to the microphone and lifted his speech, hastily written only thirty minutes ago. He choked out a nervous cough and began.

"This... this morning... Ca-Ca-Callahan, South Carolina suffered the worst tragedy and loss of life-" The press interrupted immediately.

"Have you found a culprit for today's bombing? What are you doing about the daily murders? When will the deaths stop?!" he yelled. Bailey looked like he was about to have a stroke. He wiped his forehead with his hand, soaking it with cold sweat. Fat drops of sweat fell onto the papers in his hands, slushing the words together.

"Mayor Bailey! Why hasn't the Callahan PD tracked down any of the Ghost Killers yet?" a journalist demanded.

"Pl-Please, save the questions for the end." He turned back to his speech. "We are doing everything we can to minimize the casualties today. Callahan extends its deepest thanks to nearby hospitals for taking in the injured. In the aftermath of such a tragedy, we ask for everyone's thoughts and prayers."

"Thoughts and fucking prayers?!" an onlooker roared. The crowd erupted again, drowning out the pitiful Bailey.

"Please... Please let me speak," he begged the crowd.

"Mayor Bailey! Locals say the town is cursed! They say that the Wretched Man has arrived! What is your opinion on that?" a journalist bellowed over the cacophony. Bailey slammed his hand onto the podium, silencing the crowd. He took off his glasses slowly and gazed out at the crowd with teary eyes.

"My daughter was a doctor at the hospital. She... she didn't make it."

The room fell silent.

Grace felt her heart skip a beat. "Oh my God," she whispered.

Bailey glanced at his notes and shook his head. What he'd written was pointless.

"We are doing everything we can, but everyone must remain calm. Mass panic will only make things worse. The Feds are here and they're going to take over now. Chief Laramie resigned this morning. The interim chief will be Captain Anthony York. We wish him the best of luck." He let out a long sigh, that ended in a tired cough. When he recovered, he faced the crowd with blood-shot eyes.

"I am sorry, people of Callahan. Today showed that I am clearly unable to fulfill my oath to serve Callahan. I have failed Callahan. I have failed you. I have failed my daughter. I must go home to grieve with my family. This is my resignation as mayor." Without another word, Bailey stepped away from the podium and walked out. The entire room was frozen in stunned silence.

"Jesus," Isaac breathed.

For a minute, the platform remained empty and the cameras rolled on nothing. It was absolutely bizarre. No one knew what to do.

Finally, an aide jumped to the podium and nervously gestured toward the side of the room.

"Um, Dr. Cornwall," she introduced, before slipping off the stage.

A bespectacled man in a white doctor's coat stepped up onto the podium. He put on a brave face and adjusted the microphone for his short stature. He was about sixty, with short silver hair and a perfectly manicured beard.

"Good afternoon. My name is Dr. Malcolm Cornwall and I practice in the department of psychiatry and behavioral sciences at the Medical University of South Carolina. I will only take a moment before turning it over to General Smith. Now then, in times of tragedy and loss, it is a necessity to not succumb to rapidly spreading fear. This can lead to mass hysteria. Fear breeds off fear and the results of this fear can cause great social disruption." Dr. Cornwall adjusted his glasses before continuing.

"There is no such thing as the 'Wretched Man.' There is no such thing as the devil. There is no monster, demon or ghost haunting Callahan. Anyone who supports this idea should be ashamed of themselves. What Callahan needs is rational men and women to bring it back to prosperity. This 'myth' of the Wretched Man is exactly that, a myth. A fairy tale. It is something meant to keep kids in their beds at night. In short, it is pure imagination. Witness statements are indicative that a Mass Psychogenic Illness, or mass hysteria, has plagued the populace of this city. Symptoms include paranoia, cognitive decline, occasional flu-like symptoms, such as coughing and sweats, and in exceptional cases, psychosis and hallucinations. The mind is a very powerful thing, and if you let it run wild, you get today's eyewitness accounts of the Wretched Man. Mass Hysteria is how the Salem Witch Trials happened." Dr. Cornwall leaned forward and lowered his eyebrows.

"Believe in the facts, Callahan. Do not believe in childhood nightmares. My team will be setting up practice in Callahan to provide oversight and treatment. Thank you. Stay safe." Dr. Cornwall nodded to the press before stepping away, ignoring the questions shouted at him.

General Terrence Smith immediately lumbered up to the podium. He was 60, built like a tank and dark skinned with a stare that could cut steel. His chest was emblazoned with medals, and his head was perfectly shaved to a gleaming finish. Four stars adorned his collar and his massive shoulders rippled with muscle.

He gripped the sides of the podium and leered out at the sea of press with a scowl that clearly stated, "try me." He spoke in a harsh, icy tone that had a hint of a Kentucky accent.

"This was a terrorist attack, plain and simple. We will find the culprits and eliminate them. A battalion from the National Guard has already arrived, and they will be stationed here until this city is… cleansed. We will work with what's left of the Callahan Police Department and these killings will be put to bed, end of story." General Smith leaned forward, boring his stare into anyone who dared to meet it. He jammed a finger at the press.

"I will hear no more about the 'Wretched Man' or 'curse' or 'the devil.' That is bullshit and I do not have time for it. If I deem it necessary, I will have Governor Randall enact martial law in this town. I will turn this city into Guantanamo Bay overnight if that happens. You have my word. No questions. Dismissed."

5. The Walls of Jericho

"We're feeding off the fear, and it's making us all go insane."

It was 2 a.m. when Isaac finally left Callahan PD. He stepped into the gentle night air; summer was on its way. He took a deep breath to settle his nerves. The last sixteen hours had been nothing short of hell. His stomach was shouting at him to eat something, since he hadn't had a bite since his morning omelet. As he entered the parking lot, a National Guard corporal in fatigues stepped out from the door and addressed him.

"Questioning at 8 am sharp. Don't forget, Murphy," he snapped coldly.

"Right," Isaac muttered.

"Right, *sir*," the soldier shot back.

Isaac glowered at him with a fiery stare. The young corporal flinched at the flames. He'd seen something in that gaze he wished he hadn't. Isaac turned his back to the kid and started walking towards the metro. Callahan's metro was brand new, having only been finished five years ago, back when the city was booming and the need for a public rail was in high demand. However, given the exodus of the civilian population, the trains were now often empty.

Isaac gritted his teeth in anger, because driving wasn't going to be an option for the foreseeable future. The fear of a panic attack or a hallucination while behind the wheel was enough for him to refrain from operating a vehicle. He plodded down the sidewalk and muttered, "I've already totaled my car, it ain't worth totaling Emily's, too."

He found a little peace in the still night air. It was quiet and the stars were out. For once, the city seemed to be asleep. He turned a corner and left the well-lit sidewalk behind him. After a moment, he entered a sketchier street. Several streetlamps were broken, and given the current situation of the city, they weren't likely to be repaired anytime soon. Homeless were everywhere, sleeping in doorways and even on the sidewalk. Isaac tried to avoid stepping on anyone in the dark.

"Reminds me of San Francisco," Isaac muttered. He and Emily had vacationed there two summers ago.

The metro station was only another two blocks away when Isaac noticed what seemed to be a hooded transient approaching him. Isaac could tell the young man was trouble even before he slipped out a folding knife from his dirty sleeve. Isaac brushed aside his jacket, showing off the gleaming stainless-steel slide of the Springfield, holstered to his hip. The young man's eyes grew as wide as dinner plates.

"It'll take more than that, buddy." Isaac chided. The vagrant cracked a smile and shrugged as Isaac headed passed him.

Isaac felt a buzz in his pocket and dug out his phone. It was David.

"Hey, man. You good?" Isaac asked. On the other end, David was driving his motorcycle through the city streets, on the way home. He had his phone hooked up to his helmet as usual.

"Yeah, I'm okay. I just… I just needed someone to talk to."

Isaac nodded slowly with a grimace. He turned off the sketchy street and entered the final stretch to the metro.

"I'm here. You can always talk to me."

David came to a stop at a red light and glanced to his left. Clear. Right. Clear. Up. Clear. A car pulled next to him and he settled down slightly.

"I need to ask you something… personal," David said.

Isaac held the phone a little closer to his ear and squinted.

"Of course."

David ground his teeth and looked around again with a shiver.

"This is not… normal," he struggled to get the final word out.

"Nothing in this town is. Tell me what's going on."

David took a deep breath to compose himself. The light turned green and he took off, giving the throttle a good twist to gather speed away from the dark intersection.

"Do you ever see… Emily?" David asked. Isaac froze and gripped the phone tightly. He quickened his pace and leaned in close to the phone to speak in a hushed tone.

"Yes, I do. Initially it was just for a second, like I'd hear her voice in the house or I'd see a brief glimpse of her as I turned. But now I see her just about every day. And I… I talk to her a lot."

David was silent on the other end. Isaac winced uncomfortably. Eventually, David let out a long bitter sigh.

"Damn, I didn't know it was that bad. I'm sorry, Isaac."

Isaac waved the worry away. "You know, at first it scared me. But now I… I want to see her more. I'm happy when she does show up." "*And destroyed when she disappears,*" he thought.

"Oh, man…." David didn't know where to begin. He took a turn and entered a dark stretch that wasn't illuminated and continued.

"Well, I just got out of the office and-"

"I'm sorry, again about Charlotte," Isaac cut in. "It's going to be okay."

David's face was stony. He considered ending the call but held off. He had to get this off his chest. "Thank you, but that wasn't why I was calling." David trailed off, unable to find the words.

"David?"

"Right… shit. Okay." David checked one more time, but again, saw nothing.

"I've been seeing that woman all day," he confessed.

"What woman… Oh." Isaac realized what was happening.

David nodded. He took another deep breath and blurted the rest. "When the officers brought her down from the ceiling, I could still see her hanging there. Then she just kinda *floated* there, above everyone. So, there was the corpse on the ground along with her, hanging in the air, staring at me. Later at headquarters I saw her several times while shit was going crazy. She was hanging behind officers and even above my desk."

Isaac was speechless.

"Right before I called you, I saw her in the parking lot, hanging above my motorcycle. I had just dropped off the squad car so I could take my motorcycle home, which I had left there from yesterday. I tried not to look at her. I just got on and drove off, but I know she watched me leave." David hit the throttle again, speeding up on the road. He was subconsciously trying to escape. He got choked up and coughed.

"I'm scared," he said in a voice that could have belonged to a frightened child.

"Stay with me, tonight. It's much better than being in that empty house by yourself." Isaac cursed himself for using the word 'empty.'

David coughed again. "Goddamn you, Charlotte," he spat.

"I'm sorry. I shouldn't have used that word," Isaac apologized.

"It's okay, and thanks for the invite. I think some company might help me feel better." David flicked on his turn signal and changed direction for Isaac's house.

"The woman you see, she can't hurt you," Isaac promised.

"I think she can. Remember what the witnesses have been saying for months? Remember what they said at the hospital today? Remember-"

Isaac cut him off. "I saw the O'Donnell kid in the woods the night we played poker."

David nodded morosely. "I knew something had spooked you. But we're all so high strung as it is, I didn't want to press."

"I found him in the woods. It was awful. He was just like how we found him on the street, guts all strewn out and swollen. I panicked when I saw him. On the drive home next morning, I ran him over on the street. But there was nothing there. No damage. No body. It was nothing but me, having a panic attack," Isaac explained.

"It's like that doctor said, it must be mass hysteria. We're feeding off the fear, and it's making us all go insane." David pulled up to Isaac's dark house. He parked his bike in front of the garage and stepped off.

"I just pulled into your driveway. Are you not home yet?" David asked.

Isaac glanced at the entrance to the metro in front of him.

"No, like I said, I don't want to drive. I'm hopping on the train, give me twenty minutes. You know where I keep the spare key?"

David nodded. He pulled his Glock 21 out of his side holster and kept it in his hand as he approached the front door.

"Yeah, I do. I'll just turn on the TV then." He fished around under a plank of window siding and withdrew a key. "I don't know how I'm going to be able to be alone now. I don't think I can do it, not with that.... upside-down woman watching me."

Isaac pushed his way through a turnstile. "She's in your head, David. Don't believe her. You don't need to end up like me."

"Don't say that," David snapped back.

Isaac didn't respond. David put the key in the door and entered the dark house. He flicked on the lights, clear. He laid his things down on the dining table and looked at his pistol.

"I'm about to take a shower with my Glock," he muttered.

"Well, they do work under water," Isaac replied. Both men chuckled.

"If I wake up in the guest bedroom tonight and she's hanging above me, I might put a hole in your ceiling when I shoot her," David said.

"By all means. I hit the O'Donnell kid at 60 mph and haven't seen him since!" Isaac joked.

"Thank you, Isaac. See you soon."

"Sure thing." Isaac hung up the phone and entered the metro. It was mostly empty asides from a few homeless who were milling about. A train rolled up and he stepped on.

***

Isaac glanced around the train cabin. It was almost empty, save for a few passengers. An EMT sat up at the front of cabin. He was thoroughly exhausted. He had likely spent all day dealing with victims from the hospital. Only now, at nearly 3 a.m. was he finally going home.

Isaac took a seat in the middle of the cabin. Sitting across from him was a stone-faced woman with her back to the window. She was leaning against the paneling and casting an empty gaze at Isaac. He ignored her, discomforted by her ragged clothing and stench. She was just another nut in Callahan. He peered at the back of the cabin and saw a young man, glued to his smartphone. Isaac took a slow breath and sighed as the train began to move. He closed his eyes, eager to get a few minutes of shut eye. *"Hell of a day. Shit, hell of a life."*

The young man hopped off the train at the first stop, leaving just Isaac, the EMT and the stone-faced woman. The train hit a bumpy patch on the rails, jostling Isaac uncomfortably. Unable to catch any rest, he opened his eyes. The stone-faced woman was still staring at him.

Isaac fidgeted nervously in his seat, wondering why this nutcase was still staring at him. Try as he might, he couldn't avoid her gaze. He ended up just returning the stare, gazing into her tiny black pupils. Seconds ticked by and her stare did not waver, not even a blink. Isaac was thoroughly creeped out and finally tore his gaze away. He glanced around the train looking for a distraction that could get his mind off the creepy woman.

Twenty seconds later, he could still feel her piercing stare cutting into the side of his head. He relented and peeked back at her. He looked away immediately and felt a shiver run down his spine. The woman was boring her eyes into him. Very uneasy now, Isaac looked out the window, watching as the dark streets of Callahan rushed by. It was futile though, because now he could feel her eyes stabbing into the back of his head. Isaac regrettably turned and met her gaze full on.

Her eyes *burned* into his and Isaac pulled away once more.

"Christ, lady," he exclaimed. The woman continued her ceaseless stare.

The EMT arose and hurriedly walked to Isaac. He sat down quickly next to him. The EMT studied the woman and grimaced. He nudged Isaac with an elbow to get his attention.

"Sir? Would you mind speaking with me in the next cabin?" he asked. Isaac turned to him, grateful to have someone to look at who wasn't the woman.

"I guess. But... why?" he asked. The EMT shook his head and instead pressed Isaac with urgency, doing his best not to look at the woman.

"Please."

Isaac didn't need to hear another word. He got up and followed the EMT to the next cabin with haste. The EMT shut the door and briefly glanced at the woman through the glass window. She was still staring at the place where Isaac's head had been.

"What is it?" Isaac asked. The EMT gritted his teeth and pointed at the woman.

"That woman is dead."

Isaac looked back at the woman and realized he was right.

***

Isaac gratefully walked up his lawn and opened the front door. Inside, the television was on but there was no sign of friend.

"David?" Isaac called out.

"In the bathroom!" David shouted from upstairs. Isaac dropped his stuff off and collapsed on the couch. An old black and white western was playing on the television. David had already set up a couple of beers on the coffee table. Isaac reached out to grab one but froze in place. Resting atop the ash and charred wood in the fireplace was the uncrumpled, unburned and unharmed sketch of the Wretched Man.

Isaac jumped to his feet and grabbed the paper. He heard the shower turn off and knew he only had a few moments to dispose of the sketch. He rushed upstairs to his bedroom and grabbed a Bible from a shelf. Without looking at the sketch, he shoved the sketch in between the holy pages. He ran to his closet and tied the bible shut with a belt, before locking the whole mess into his safe. The bathroom door opened, and David stepped out.

"Isaac?" David called as Isaac left his bedroom.

"There you are. Shit bout time."

David and Isaac headed downstairs and took their seats.

"Thanks for letting me stay over," David added.

"Of course. Now, what's with these beers? We have to be back at the station in five hours for interviews."

David chuckled and grabbed two bottles. "Bud, Callahan will either be 'cured' or it's going to burn to the ground. They can't fire us; they need all hands-on deck. So, get drunk with me."

"You always knew how to get me to indulge in my vices," Isaac muttered.

David grinned and handed Isaac a beer. The two clinked bottles and began the serious business of getting wasted.

***

As the sun rose on the city of Callahan, so did its terrified inhabitants. Another night of misery and murder had warmed up the city for another day of savagery.

The protestors, hundreds deep, pounded main street in defiance against the National Guard takeover. People chanted, screamed and fought amongst one another. Large signs and effigies of the Wretched Man bobbed in and out of the crowd. Someone tossed a Molotov cocktail through a recruitment office, sending a terrified soldier onto the street, ripping his burning camouflage jacket off in a panic. Windows were shattered and a police car was set ablaze. A line of riot police arrived, National Guard reinforcements, and they beat back the protestors.

Outsiders from all over the country streamed down Interstate 77 and 26 to enter the city. Callahan National Airport flooded with arrivals, eager to sightsee in the *Cursed City of Callahan*. Nihilistic anarchists, clad in all black with facemasks, slipped into the protests, eager to join the violence.

Meanwhile, Callahan natives were desperate to escape before they wound up on the chopping block. Every house, every family, every parent or sibling had a friend who was dead, a father who committed suicide, or a niece who had been butchered.

A moving truck, packed to the brim, drove along a neighborhood street; every house it passed had a "For Sale" sign planted in the front yard. Their prices had been slashed once, slashed twice and even three times. It didn't matter. Those houses could be free and not a soul would take them. Tears were shed as families left the city with nowhere to go, mortgages to pay and bankruptcy all but guaranteed.

Transients, once a rare sight in Callahan, now swamped the

streets, begging for food or money. They blamed their misfortune on the Wretched Man.

A teenager twirled in little circles underneath a low-hanging lamp post. Pedestrians walked by, indifferent to the belt around his neck, either too depressed or too terrified to care.

A librarian, her throat slashed from chin to collarbone, slumped at the front desk of the city library. Somebody had walked right up and stabbed her with a fish knife in broad daylight. Isaac and David looked at her corpse with desensitized eyes. Grace wiped her eyes and moved on with her duties. Isaac just shook his head. David hadn't slept in days and was in a downward spiral.

The city morgue was overflowing with a long wait time for new autopsies. Callahan Cemetery filled its last plot and conducted its final burial. Tears fell and the color black was everywhere.

Callahan PD had been enveloped by military barricades, tents and towers. This was headquarters for the National Guard and General Smith was working in tandem with Chief York. Pale with enormous dark circles under his eyes, York looked to be on death's door from the stress. Smith was taking it better, but even his powerful hands shook.

***

A month later, Isaac and Grace slumped at their desks. It was 10 p.m. and they were weary to the bone. David trudged up to them with a few mugs of hot green tea threaded in his fingers. Everyone took a mug and had a few grateful sips.

"Look on the positive side, at least we're all getting a raise!" Grace exclaimed.

"It's wonderful, all this money I'm getting has made me so happy," Isaac replied sarcastically.

Grace frowned.

"Well, you may not care, but it certainly helps me. I'm still paying off my student loans. Though I'd honestly work here for free."

"As would I," Isaac said. "It is surprising that they can keep paying us at all. With so many residents moving out, tax revenues have plummeted. City hall is so entrenched in debt that even if we stop the killings, it would take years for Callahan to climb out of its financial hole. The only thing keeping us afloat right now are the grants from the government and disaster funds."

"Well, having a city all over the news collapse isn't good for optics. The census recorded that Callahan had 500,000 residents, too big to fail. Uncle Sam is very keen on keeping the cash flowing," David grumbled.

A distant scream filled the air and David peered out a window towards the street. "More and more protestors every day. One day they're gonna overturn the barricade and trample over the National Guard."

Grace turned to Isaac.

"Have you heard anything about Johnson's progress?" she asked.

Isaac shook his head.

"Well, he says he might have something. He's planning on presenting it to York tomorrow," Grace said enthusiastically.

"Just another dead end," David muttered dryly.

Isaac looked into his mug, feeling the steam warm his face. He closed his eyes and took a deep calming breath.

"Please, David. Optimism is key," Grace advised.

David tapped the window and indicated the sea of increasingly violent protestors. "Yeah. Because it's all we have right now," he muttered glumly.

A pair of footsteps approached from the hallway and a moment later Chief York walked in. He sat down heavily by the trio.

"Hey, Chief," Isaac greeted.

York took off his glasses and rubbed his tired face. He'd lost a good ten pounds since he'd been made chief.

"How long are you going to stick it out?" Isaac asked.

York looked up, angry that anyone thought he would abandon his position. Then, he softened and cracked a small smile.

"Y'know, all my life I've wanted to be Callahan's Chief of Police. I've been in this department since I became a probationary officer at 21. My father was a captain and my mother worked in forensics. But now I'm here and I've never hated work more."

Isaac offered York his mug and York gratefully took a long sip of tea before continuing.

"Thanks. But no, I'm not leaving. I was born in Callahan and I'll die here too."

A rattle of distant gunfire reverberated through the air and David peered out the window.

"A protestor climbed the barricade and pulled a gun. They shot her," he said.

York rubbed his temples.

"Christ. That's going to be a lot of paperwork. I'll just add it to the mountain on my desk. The press is going to have a field day."

David slurped down the rest of his tea and stood up.

"I'm headed out," he said. "See y'all tomorrow."

York stood up as well and bid his goodbye before following David out.

Grace flipped open a case file, but Isaac reached out and closed it shut.

"Leave it for tomorrow morning, best to get some sleep while you can. Come on."

Grace started to argue, but realized Isaac was right. The two packed up and headed for the parking lot. Grace unlocked her car and Isaac hopped into the passenger seat.

"I appreciate you playing chauffeur, Grace," he said. "I must say, I feel like a bum carpooling with you or David."

"Don't worry about it," Grace smiled. "You're on the way and it's better to drive in pairs these days anyway."

They drove in companionable silence until they reached Isaac's house. Isaac got out and walked around to the driver's side window. Grace rolled it down.

"Yes?" she asked.

Isaac gripped the window and stared Grace in the eyes.

"You should pack your things tonight and go back to Charleston," he stated.

Grace's face scrunched up in surprise.

"Absolutely not! This city needs me, and I'd never forgive myself if I left-"

Isaac cut her off. "David and I are hopeless and stuck. We've accepted it. I need to get revenge on the man who killed my wife. I have nothing else to live for. But you still have optimism and hope. I don't want to see that get swallowed up by this city. You're going to end up disillusioned like us... or dead."

Grace was silent for a moment. She gripped the steering wheel and spoke seriously.

"You told me that you promised Emily you'd save this city."

When Isaac didn't answer, she stared into his eyes and he was taken aback by her resolve.

"This city needs people like me, people who still have hope. Because that is the only thing that will save Callahan from doom. But I can't do it by myself. I need someone like you who has the experience-" Grace tapped Isaac's chest with a knuckle "-and the courage to fight. So, goodnight, Isaac." Grace rolled up her window and drove away.

Isaac couldn't help but to smile ever so slightly. "She could give you a run for your money, Emily."

***

A press conference at city hall, led by General Smith, was underway. Dimly, one could hear the shouts of protestors outside. The name *Jamie Robbins* was heard in the chants; she was the woman who had been shot at the barricade. Isaac and David were in attendance and stood at the back of the room behind all the press. A large projector hung from the ceiling and flashed the bullet points of the day's briefing on a white wall behind General Smith. He cleared his throat and grabbed the microphone.

"A month has passed since the National Guard was deployed to Callahan and we are working around the clock to keep the public safe. I want to thank the Callahan PD for its hard work, particularly from its new police chief, Anthony York." Smith gestured toward York, who was seated in the front row. A painfully weak smattering of applause filled the air in response.

"Now then," Smith continued.

"General Smith," a journalist cut in. "Will you ask Governor Randall to declare martial law?"

Before he could answer, a reporter interrupted, "General Smith, do you have any further comments on the death of Jamie Robbins? Or the lawsuit that her family has brought against Callahan?"

"General! The murder rate has only increased in the month since you took over! What is your opinion on that?" another asked.

General Smith pounded his hand against the podium. "Quiet! One at a time!" He set his sights upon the first journalist.

"You!" he commanded.

She nodded. "Martial law?"

"When I deem it necessary."

"And when will that-"

General Smith cut her off with a blazing retort. "I will make that decision! And the first thing I'll do if that happens is throw you and any other annoying journalists in irons!" The young journalist shrank back in terror. General Smith switched his attention to the next journalist and shot him a poisonous glower. "What?" he demanded.

The man raised a nicotine-stained finger.

"Well sir, do you have any further comments on the murder of Jamie Robbins."

General Smith crossed his arms and snorted, as if that question were beneath him. "For the tenth time, her death was an avoidable tragedy. Going over the barricades is illegal and subject to immediate arrest but drawing a firearm on a soldier is subject to immediate lethal force. My soldiers were following policy. The only person at fault in her death is her. Next question!"

The callousness of Generals Smith's answer briefly stunned the audience. After a moment, a veteran African American reporter raised his hand. General Smith pointed at him. In a voice familiar to millions, he asked, "General Smith, you say that you are 'working around the clock' and are pleased with the work of the Callahan PD, yet the murder rate for last month was the worst it has ever been. Can you comment?" he asked.

General Smith's lips tightened, baring yellowed teeth.

"You can't make an omelet without breaking a few eggs. Rest assured, we are nearing a breakthrough."

The reporter narrowed his eyes.

"Would you care to enlighten us about this 'breakthrough?'" he asked. General Smith ignored him and pointed to another reporter.

"You!" he commanded. The woman jumped at the opportunity.

"Are there any updates on the Ghost Killers? What about the popular opinion that they aren't real? Can you provide any evidence one way or another? What are the detectives at Callah-"

General Smith interrupted her angrily.

"One question at a time, dammit! Now," he cracked his knuckles and delivered what everyone knew was a bald-faced lie. "Rest assured, the Ghost Killers are real, and my officers are closer than ever to apprehending the sons of bitches." He leaned across the podium and cast a stink eye at everyone.

One brave journalist spoke up.

"General Smith, reports of the Wretched Man-" A shiver swept the whole crowd.

Isaac felt a tingle travel down his spine.

"Christ," he muttered.

The journalist glanced around nervously but continued, "Ummm, right… General Smith, reports about the… thing… are happening daily. Do you truly believe there isn't even a shred of fact to them? There have been thousands of eyewitness statements at this point."

General Smith waved his hand as if he were passing off a trivial matter.

"Statements from thousands of liars, or assholes off their meds. Don't waste my time."

A balding journalist pressed forward immediately. "General Smith, you can't just write off thousands of reports! What about the death of Dr. Cornwall last week? Eyewitnesses said the Wretched Man tore him apart!"

General Smith swiped at his microphone, causing a squeal of feedback. He stared viciously at the journalist with fire in his eyes. "I have had enough of this nonsense! The Wretched Man is bullshit! He is a goddamn fairytale! There is not a goddamn thing that-"

A gasp from the crowd interrupted his rant.

"What the hell is that?" a reporter gaped. She pointed at the ceiling. "Oh my God!" she cried. Everyone's eyes followed her gaze. Isaac squinted at the tiled ceiling.

A bloody face was hanging from a gap in the tiles.

"What in the hell," General Smith whispered.

The area around the face bent and broke apart. The mangled corpse crashed down, flattening a poor sound technician. The crowd erupted into screams.

General Smith's eyes widened as he stared at the mass of pipes and wiring visible through the hole in the ceiling. "There's someone up there! Ghost Killer! *Open Fire!*" He ripped his Sig Sauer P226 pistol out of his hip holster and unloaded into the ceiling. A shower of tile rained onto the press and spectators.

A bullet struck the cables of the big projector, and it groaned, before plummeting directly into the crowd. It crushed a female journalist immediately. Its metal edge caught a cameraman on the side of head, shearing off a chunk of his skull. He crumpled to the ground as brain matter and blood spilled all over him. Another bullet ricocheted off a pipe and nailed a city official in the shoulder.

Isaac rushed to the stage and tackled General Smith, wrenching the gun from Smith's hand, but not before the general accidentally sent another round directly into the crowd, hitting an intern in the stomach.

"Stop fucking shooting!" Isaac screamed as he and General Smith landed in a heap.

In the news control room, stunned producers forgot to cut the live feed, so all of America got to watch the blood bath on live television.

In complete panic, the crowd bolted for the exits, causing a stampede. A man was trampled after he tripped over a chair, blinded by blood from a gash on his forehead. A woman, holding the corpse that had fallen from the ceiling, cried out in despair, "Claws! The Wretched Man shredded her alive!"

Several people smashed into the active cameraman flipping the camera and finally cutting the feed. Isaac wiped his stinging eyes. Dust from the collapsed ceiling had fallen and was starting to clog the air. Isaac could barely see anything amidst the haze. He got off General Smith, who was staring at his hands in shock.

"What have I done?" General Smith whispered as if he could actually see the innocent blood on them.

Isaac rose to his feet and looked around the haze. Dust entered his lungs and he coughed violently to clear it. With watering eyes, he stared at the wounded and dead. Isaac stepped forward to help, only to slip on a pool of blood and fall awkwardly to his knees.

"Oof!" he cried out. He rose again slowly as the stampeding crowd broke down the closed door, spilling light into the room.

"David?" he called out as he squinted into the emptying room. He saw David and rushed forward to where his friend was lying in fetal position.

"David!" he exclaimed. But David couldn't hear him, he was catatonic, staring at something through the dust in pure horror. Isaac followed his gaze into the dust and squinted.

"Is that...." Isaac breathed. He shook his head and turned back to David, who was hyperventilating.

"She's not real, David! But these people are! Please help me!" he begged.

David didn't respond, even when Isaac tried to pull him to his feet. Isaac tried to pull away, desperate to help others, but David grabbed his hand with an iron grip.

"Please don't leave me," David begged.

Isaac tried again to pull away but couldn't escape the grip.

"David, please, we have to help." Isaac collapsed into a coughing fit.

***

At a nondescript bar on the outskirts of Callahan, Isaac nursed a shot of whiskey and gazed out the window at the night sky. His head was cradled in his hand as he drifted in and out of focus. An old timey jukebox cranked out classic rock as Isaac stared at his whiskey, which was clearly not his first.

The bartender slipped out from the backroom, and the wooden floor creaked under his heavy boot tread. A rustic pump-action shotgun was slung over his shoulder and a fat cigar hung from his lips. He stroked his grey beard and gave Isaac a quizzical look. "I'm shutting it down in five minutes," he said in a smoker's rasp, and Isaac downed the whiskey.

The bartender pulled out two shot glasses and filled them both up with scotch. "Here, last one's on me. It's the good stuff," he muttered. He knocked his shot back and took a good look around his bar.

"I ain't opening this place again until when and if this city ever gets out of this rotten mess. Damn shame. Not too long ago, this place was always packed. And now… haven't had more than a dozen customers in a week for months."

He glanced at Isaac, who wasn't paying much attention.

"No offense, partner, but they all looked just like you."

Isaac grabbed the whiskey and threw it back, grimacing. He let out a dry heave. The bartender reached for the shot glass tentatively.

"Maybe you've had enough," the bartender said.

But Isaac snatched the shot glass from him.

"I'm fine. I need it. Pour me another. I'll pay extra," he hissed. The bartender shrugged and poured another.

Isaac slowly raised his head to look the bartender in the eye, ignoring his growing headache.

"Why haven't you left?" he asked.

The bartender chuckled.

"I could ask you the same question." He looked around his place almost lovingly, before resting a hand on the wood-paneled bar. "Callahan's my home. My Pa built this bar. I grew up here. It was my childhood. So, I'll be damned if I run away with my tail between my legs, Wretched Man or not."

"So, you believe in him?" Isaac asked.

The bartender swung his shotgun off his shoulder and rubbed a hand down its shining steel barrel.

"Ghosts and devils don't scare me, people do."

The bartender glanced behind himself at a mounted television that was playing the nightly news on mute. He grabbed a remote and turned up the volume. A replay of the disastrous news conference was being broadcasted while a pair of anchors delved into General Smith's background. The bartender pointed at the television with the remote.

"Mark my words, General Smith killed more people today than any fairytale did."

One of the news anchors launched into a monologue.

"General Smith was placed under arrest immediately after these events transpired. But he will first be admitted for a psychiatric evaluation to determine if he is suffering from severe PTSD. Analysts say he will likely be charged with numerous counts of involuntary manslaughter and reckless endangerment. South Carolina Governor, Randall, has already announced his replacement, the celebrated General Alison Grey, who has taken command."

Isaac gulped as footage of General Grey's speech played. The bartender raised a grizzled eyebrow.

"You know her?" he asked.

Isaac shrugged.

"Not really, but some of my fellow detectives served under her before joining the force. She's… cruel. Had a hell of a track record in the Middle East."

The two men watched as General Grey stepped behind a podium. She was a sharp-featured woman in her early sixties, sporting a salt and pepper buzz cut. Her dark eyes were cold and unforgiving. Her skin was acne scarred and uncomfortably pale.

"Callahan is sick," she began, "and I will cure it. Desperate times call for desperate measures. Under my authority, the 'Ghost Killers' will be eliminated. Governor Randall has given me the authority to enact martial law in Callahan and I fully intend to follow through. When that does happen, anyone caught out after curfew will be arrested, or worse. If the Ghost Killers are to be found, we must be more brutal than they are."

A journalist raised a hand and asked a question.

"General Grey, your track record in the Middle East was controversial to say the least. We all know about your… nickname… Would you care to comment on whether or not you think you are the right choice to lead Callahan?" she asked.

General Grey smiled and it was a chilling sight, because not a shred of emotion reached her eyes. It was as if the top of her face was made of wax. It didn't help that her teeth were yellow and unseemly sharp.

"There's a reason the Taliban nicknamed me 'Pale Death.' My methods are considered by some to be vile, but they get the job done. That is why Governor Randall chose me for the job. I get results. Make no mistake, monsters are killing Callahan. And the best way to kill a monster is with an even more vicious monster."

The bartender shuddered.

"Christ, that woman is terrifying," he muttered. He then glanced over at Isaac. "So, you're a detective, huh?" He looked Isaac up and down and suddenly recognized him.

"Aw, shit! You're the one who tackled General Smith! Detective Murphy!"

Isaac didn't look up. He instead knocked back the scotch and placed it down with a thud. It echoed throughout the bar dully.

"This city is cursed," Isaac stated emptily.

The bartender shrugged. "Perhaps."

Isaac was silent. The bartender glanced back at the television, where the news was again replaying the press conference disaster.

"Six dead and two dozen wounded by gunshots and the resulting stampede. That room was absolutely packed to the brim. Hey," he leaned in close to Isaac. "What was it like in there amidst all that?"

Isaac stood up and threw some money on the bar.

"Thanks for the scotch," he said shortly. He turned his back on the bartender and left.

***

Isaac, washed out and drunk, was slumped against a bench in the metro station, waiting for the next train to arrive. Several overhead lights in the station had gone out and it was unlikely they'd be fixed anytime soon; the repairman left town permanently two weeks ago. Isaac shut his eyes and leaned his head back, exhausted.

"Hey! Hey, mister!" a shrill voice rang out.

Isaac cracked open his bloodshot eyes and glared at the voice who had called out to him. Standing on the tracks beneath Isaac, was a homeless man. He was covered in dirt and, unsettlingly, a fair amount of dried blood. He grinned at Isaac, showing off his three brown teeth. The man pressed himself up against the wall that bordered the train tracks, so all Isaac could see was his bald head floating in the darkness. The vagrant eyed Isaac's badge that was clipped to his belt, and grinned.

"Hee-hee, Mr. Police! Drinking on the job? Tut-tut!" the vagrant teased.

"Piss off," Isaac grumbled. The vagrant giggled again.

"My name's Billy, what's yours, Mr. Police?" Billy badgered. When Isaac didn't respond, Billy jumped up and down with a throaty cackle.

"Aw, not a big talker, eh?"

Isaac checked the time schedule. The train was due in three minutes. It couldn't come soon enough.

"Say, you haven't seen my friend, Stevie, have you?" Billy asked. Isaac ignored him, and Billy pouted. Isaac noticed a particularly large open sore on the side of Billy's face. It was leaking white pus.

"Drat! Haven't seen hide or tail of him since he went to go talk to the eight-fingered man," Billy muttered.

Isaac's ears perked up. *"Eight fingers."*

Isaac sobered up immediately and leaned forward, adrenaline coursing through his veins.

"Eight-fingered man? What does he look like?" Isaac demanded.

Billy shrugged. "I've never met him! And I hope I never do, because he keeps mooching Stevie from me!"

Isaac pressed him further. "It's very important to me. Do you know where I can find him?"

Billy ignored him and looked around anxiously.

"What I need to *find* is Stevie. Stevie! Yoo'hoo!" He turned heel and traipsed off into the darkness. Isaac stood at the edge of the platform, squinting in an effort to see something in the dark night. The tracks went into an underground train tunnel that was undoubtably filled with homeless, but Isaac couldn't see anything.

"Hey! Where'd you go?" Isaac shouted. There was no answer; however, in the distance Billy began calling out for Stevie in a sing-song voice, similar to a child singing to a play doll.

"Steeviee! Yoo'hoo! Where are you?" Billy's voice echoed.

Isaac gave up on trying to see anything in the darkness. He returned to the bench and sat down, to gather his thoughts. Suddenly, distant clapping filled the air. Billy had found Stevie.

"Stevie!! There you are! How's my little Stevie doing?" Billy's voice echoed.

Billy's footsteps preceded him as he approached the station on the tracks. A moment later, his head popped up once more from the top of the wall. He was grinning from ear to ear.

"Look who I found!" he exclaimed. Stevie's head came into view next to Billy's.

"It's Stevie!" Billy sang with joy.

Isaac examined Stevie. He didn't look healthy. His mouth was hanging open as Billy chortled with laughter and his tongue lolled to one side. Isaac instinctively reached his hand for his holstered Glock 21.

"Say hi to our new friend, Stevie!"

Stevie's head rose into the air, just his head because he had no body. Billy, holding the severed head by the back of the hair, shook Stevie up and down with excitement. A piece of bloody viscera squished in between Billy's fingers and splatted on the ground. Isaac recoiled in horror.

"Aw, a little shy, Stevie? That's okay. Our friend Mr. Police is shy, too! I'm sure you two will become the best of friends!"

Isaac drew his Glock 21 and aimed it right at Billy's forehead.

"You're… you're under arrest," Isaac stammered.

Billy's eyes grew wide at the sight of the black pistol. He grinned big and brown as the station filled with light.

"Goodbye, Mr. Police," he whispered.

Shriek! The train conductor slammed the whistle. Isaac jumped at the noise and turned for a second to the oncoming train. When he looked back, Billy was gone, although he could hear rapidly fading footsteps heading towards the tunnel.

Stunned, Isaac shakily holstered his pistol and approached the bus. He stumbled inside and sat down heavily next to a window. He scanned the darkness outside but saw no sign of Billy or the severed head. With a ding, the train doors closed, and Isaac was on his way.

***

Isaac was lying in bed, cradling Emily's portrait. He took a slow, troubled breath and raised the photo in the half-light so he could see Emily's beautiful green eyes.

"I love you, baby… so much." He kissed the photo and felt a wave of grief wash over him. He laid there for an hour, unable to escape into sleep.

His phone rang suddenly from the floor next to him. On the fourth ring, Isaac managed to pick it up and bring it to his ear.

"David?" Isaac choked.

Meanwhile, David was lying in bed as well, with an AR-15 rifle in his hands as he stared around his well-lit bedroom.

"Isaac," he said in a voice filled with terror. "She's in the house with me. I can hear her. Please come over here as soon as possible. Please, I'm begging you. I'm... scared."

Isaac looked at the clock, it was 2 a.m. He then looked back at Emily's eyes.

"Can you come here, instead?" Isaac asked.

David's eyes grew wide. "No. I don't want to open my bedroom door," he insisted. "She's going to be... hanging right there in the hallway. I know it. I can't face her. I can't."

Isaac looked once more at Emily, wanting nothing more than to close his eyes and sleep with her.

"She's not real, David. Open your door and face her," he stated.

"She's real to me. Isaac... please," David pleaded.

Isaac shut his eyes. "Don't be afraid of her."

"Like you're not afraid of the Wretched Man? You check your shoulders recently?" David retorted with malice flashing across his face.

Isaac grimaced and spoke without hesitation. "Goodnight, David."

David recoiled, terror returning to his face. "Isaac, wait! I'm sorry! Please! I'm sorry! Please don't-" Isaac hung up and tossed his phone onto the carpet, overcome with a myriad of emotions. He wept onto the portrait of Emily until he fell asleep.

6. It Takes a Monster

"The ends will justify the means,"

In his dream, Isaac and Emily were cuddling in their bed on a chilly December night. Through the large window across from them, they could see the vast starry sky. Bare branches swayed in the wind, but they were warm and safe beneath the covers.

"Can you feel her?" Emily whispered into Isaac's ear. He gently placed his palm onto her large belly. He almost immediately felt a little nudge. He smiled, completely content, and kissed Emily passionately.

"I do."

***

Isaac sat at his desk, furiously working on his first legitimate lead in months. Next to him, a mountain of untouched paperwork was waiting to be dealt with, but Isaac ignored it. He peeked over at Grace, who was helping him with the lead, before continuing to examine the evidence photo that was taken the night Emily was killed: the two severed fingers.

"There's no chance that he's a Ghost Killer?" Grace asked.

Isaac ground his teeth.

"Unlikely. But this case is no longer cold. I have a name, a demographic and possible locations."

"It's a long shot for sure, going on the word of a homeless guy, carrying a decapitated head - We should be investigating that murder, too." Grace said. Isaac flicked his hand as if to brush away the idea.

"The murder of a transient isn't exactly a priority. But if we happen to run into... Billy... we can arrest him on suspicion. Now then..." Isaac held up a map of Callahan with two circled areas.

"Billy said he knew of an 'eight-fingered man.' That means he is either homeless himself, or a drug dealer. The largest homeless concentrations are at these two locations: inside the north subway tunnel and here." Isaac pointed at a squared-off section of west Callahan. Grace narrowed her eyes.

"You want us to go into the most dangerous parts of the city, including murder hotspots and heroin dens, and start questioning homeless on whether or not they know of an "eight-fingered man?" Grace asked.

Isaac bit his tongue. "It's the only lead I've ever had on Emily's killer. I *have* to investigate it. I have to find him," Isaac stated. He glared darkly at the photo of the severed fingers. Grace saw his glare and shivered.

She reached out and touched his arm, breaking his focus, "Isaac, I'm happy to help you find him. But you need to promise me that if we do, you won't do anything, drastic," she said. Isaac balled his hands into fists.

"No. I can't. If you don't want to help, it's okay. Taking detectives off the Ghost Killer hunt is not what this city needs."

Grace glanced at her notes. "Perhaps investigating this will lead us to some bigger answers. If anything, the homeless are an untapped demographic that might have valuable information."

Isaac gave a half smile. "Jesus, you're a nerd," he said.

Grace rubbed her face to hide her embarrassment.

"York won't approve an investigation for cases not directed towards the Ghost Killers, so it'll just be the three of us. By the way, where is David?"

Isaac's heart skipped a beat as he remembered his harsh treatment the night before.

"Christ! I need to call him." He quickly speed-dialed David.

It rung and rung. Finally, David picked up, but Isaac heard nothing but silence.

"David?" he asked. There was a long pause.

"Isaac."

A wave of relief washed over Isaac.

"I'm sorry about last night. I wasn't in a good place. Are you okay? You coming to work?" he asked.

There was another long break.

"I quit, told York I'm out. I'm getting out of the city. I can't take it anymore. I need to clear my head. Sorry, Isaac." David's voice was utterly emotionless.

Isaac took a deep breath and let it out.

"I understand. I'm just glad you're okay," he said.

"I've just been... beaten down. It's too much for one man to bare," David continued in his eerie monotone.

A twinge of dread trickled down Isaac's spine. "You should go to your folks' house. Spend a few weeks with them and recover. Don't they live in-"

"Charleston."

"Yeah... they moved down there, I remember. Good then. Well, give me a call once you... get some rest. Okay?"

"Okay," David promised.

"Goodbye, buddy." Isaac said. David hung up. Isaac stared at his phone, worried.

"David quit?" Grace asked, concerned.

Isaac turned to her and nodded.

***

Grace parked the cruiser on the side of a dilapidated street. A few homeless milled about under a light drizzle. Grace turned to Isaac with pursed lips. Isaac sighed and grabbed his raincoat.

"Let's go."

He put on his coat, pulling up the hood as he stepped from the cruiser. Instinctively, he tapped the butt of his Glock 21.

Grace locked the cruiser and gave Isaac a small nod. The two approached the nearest homeless person, an elderly woman, huddled under a bus stop. She was muttering herself.

Isaac approached her gently and tapped his badge. "Ma'am? Could I have a word?" he asked. She didn't look at him. Isaac couldn't make out what she was rapidly muttering.

"Ma'am?" he repeated, leaning in a little closer to hear.

"Round and Round the Bobbit Rock. Got to get to the top. Once you make it to the end, The Wretched Man will be your friend! Round and Round the Bobbit Rock…."

Isaac grimaced and backed away from her. Grace shook her head and pointed to a group up the street. They walked quickly through the strengthening rain towards several people, crowded under an awning.

"Da hell do dey want?" a stocky, Irish, man shouted aggressively as Isaac and Grace approached. Isaac held out a hand to stop Grace and exchanged glances with the Irish man.

"We were hoping to ask you a few-"

"Kiss my arse! Fuck off if yeh know wha's good for yeh! Fuckin Pigs!"

Isaac and Grace backed up, deescalating the possible threat. As they walked away, the man continued to yell at them.

Once out of earshot of the crowd, Grace spoke up.

"Isaac-"

Isaac cut her off. "This isn't safe at all," he said. "You should head back. I'll go on without you. Take the cruiser. I'll hop on a train home after I find something."

Grace stood stock-still and looked him in the eye.

"Absolutely not," she stated.

Isaac chuckled ruefully. "Never mind, then."

The two continued to the next block where the sidewalk was teeming with homeless and trash. It resembled a third world country.

"Keep your hand on your gun. Don't draw it but be ready for the need," Isaac said, resting his hand on the butt of his pistol. Grace shivered and did the same. A rattle of thunder cracked the air and the rain became a downpour. The two detectives ventured forward, nonetheless.

A violent scream to their right made them both jump in surprise. A vicious brawl had broken out in an alleyway. A lone man was being beaten down by several thugs. He was on the ground in fetal position, trying to protect his head from the blows.

Grace took a step into the alleyway, but Isaac held out his hand.

"Don't, it's not our fight," he warned.

"Not our fight? We're the police. Every fight is our fight!" she swore.

Isaac shook his head.

"You want to get jumped going in there? It's too dangerous when we don't have backup. Besides, he could be the bad guy, y'know?"

Grace shot Isaac a nasty glare.

"Is this how you're going to save Callahan? Letting people get murdered in an alleyway? Emily would never have supported that."

Grace's words were like a slap across the face. Isaac gritted his teeth and pushed past her. He marched right up to the group, drew his pistol and leveled it all of them.

"Stop!" he ordered.

"Shit! Pigs!" one of the men exclaimed. They saw the muzzle of his pistol and took off running. Isaac lowered his pistol, and Grace did the same. The beaten man looked up with a bloody smile.

"Hell, you saved my life! Thank you."

Isaac and Grace knelt next to the man, who was dusting himself off.

"Are you okay?" Grace asked. "What were they attacking you for?"

The man inspected himself and other than a cut lip and a black eye, he was fine. He combed a hand through his blonde hair and scratched his whiskered face. He couldn't have been more than twenty.

"I think I'm okay. And, well, because I stole their-" he looked over at a soiled backpack lying in a puddle. "Well, hot damn! They ran off without taking it!"

He scurried to the bag and unzipped it, revealing several syringes, squares of foil and plastic bags. Grace, revolted, stepped away, but Isaac was unflinching and watched the man get ready to shoot up.

Isaac pressed him with a question.

"I helped you, now you help me. I'm looking for someone people call 'the eight-fingered man.' Does that ring a bell?" Isaac said, while pulling out the police sketch for visual reference.

The junkie wasn't really listening. He wrapped a tourniquet around his arm and got a dirty syringe ready. He was quite literally going to shoot up in a filthy alley, in the rain, right after he'd been beaten bloody.

Isaac pressed again.

"Hey! I just saved your life. Are you listening?"

The junkie looked up sheepishly.

"Nah, sorry, that doesn't ring a bell." He clicked a lighter under the foil of heroin and it started bubbling.

Isaac asked again.

"He's a murderer. Please, anything?" he pleaded.

The junkie chuckled as he filled the syringe.

"We're all murderers, bud. I just blame it on the Wretched Man." He held out a track marked arm and poked an angry sore that was festering on top of a large vein in the crease of his elbow.

"Yeah, I can hit this one again for sure," he whispered. He plunged the needle as Isaac stood up in fury. The man leaned back with a sigh. "Say, y'all ain't gonna, arrest me, are ya?" he whispered, already a hundred miles away.

Isaac turned his back on the junkie and walked away.

For the next hour, Isaac and Grace met similar dead ends. Everyone they approached was either hostile, high, drunk, or couldn't be bothered. There were corpses too, many corpses. At one point the two detectives had to step over a dead man. His chest was ripped to shreds as if an animal had clawed him apart.

"Ghost Killer," Grace muttered.

"Wretched Man," Isaac returned.

Grace shivered fiercely, soaked to the bone. She put out a hand to stop Isaac. "We're going to get pneumonia if we stay out here any longer," she warned.

Isaac nodded and the two headed back. He swore silently to himself. This effort had been another failure. A block from the cruiser, Isaac noticed a young vagrant sitting in the shadows of an alleyway. He did a double take.

"I think I recognize that guy," Isaac whispered.

He did recognize him, but from where? Isaac racked his brain, trying to put a memory to the face. The young man, practically a kid, met Isaac's stare and smiled. He pulled out a shining knife and Isaac's memory clicked. He smiled back and tapped his Glock.

"It'll take more than that, buddy!" Isaac called out.

The kid chuckled and stood up. Isaac approached him as Grace stared in surprise.

"Isaac, he has a knife."

"I know. But I've got a gun."

Isaac walked up to the kid and fished out his wallet. He dug out all the cash and held it in the air. The kid's eyes grew wide.

"I've got a question to ask. If you can answer it, this cash is yours."

The kid sneered. "Paper up front!"

Isaac took out $100 and threw it on the ground.

"There's half."

The kid dove on the money and stuffed it into his pocket. He pointed his knife at Isaac's chest. "Fine, what is it?" he asked.

Isaac gave him a level gaze and pulled out the police sketch.

"I'm looking for a guy known as the 'eight-fingered-man.' Do you know where I can find him?"

The kid lowered his eyebrows and said nothing. Seconds passed as the two stood in the heavy rain. Isaac sighed and put away the money. He walked to the cruiser, where Grace was waiting, gun still drawn.

"Hey! Detective!" the kid shouted.

Isaac turned with a glimmer of hope in his eyes.

The kid walked from the alleyway and stopped just short of the cruiser. He bit his lip and shuffled his feet a little. Grace felt a pang of grief in her heart. This kid was probably no more than fifteen and all alone on the streets. The kid looked at Isaac thoughtfully.

"A friend of mine used to talk about a smack dealer who went by the name 'Eight.' Could be the same guy."

Isaac took a step forward - a step too close.

"Isaac," Grace warned.

Isaac held back, realizing his potentially costly mistake. He'd already holstered his gun. The kid noticed the blunder with a little smirk and a twirl of his knife.

"Where can I find him?" Isaac asked. The kid shrugged.

"No idea. My friend was close to him though."

Isaac cocked his head.

"Was?" he asked.

The kid snorted.

"Well, my friend's dead now so there goes your lead."

Isaac nodded and fished out the money.

"Here, as promised. Sorry to hear about your friend." Isaac tossed the other hundred on the ground. The kid picked it up with a creepy smile. Grace leaned forward from the driver's side door of the cruiser.

"What happened to your friend?" she asked.

"Wretched Man?" Isaac quipped. The kid shook his head.

"Oh, no, none of that. I killed him. It was fun," he said blankly.

Grace's jaw dropped, but Isaac nodded and got inside the cruiser, locking the doors as he did.

"Get out of the rain, kid, you'll catch a cold," Isaac said, before rolling up the window.

Grace hit the gas and the two took off. She peered into the rearview mirror at the unblinking kid until he was out of sight. He never moved from the middle of the rain-soaked street.

***

Back at the station, Isaac hit the locker room and let a hot shower drive away the bone chilling cold the rain had wrapped him in. Even under the pouring water, he could hear shouts of protestors. He swore they got louder every day. The roads leading to Callahan PD were so clogged with protestors that Grace had barely been able to drive through.

Once clean and warm, he dressed in fresh slacks, dress shirt, and tie and headed upstairs to his desk. His phone was ringing as he approached.

"Yeah?" he asked when he picked it up.

York's raspy voice came over the line.

"Isaac, it's York. Come to my office, please."

Isaac left his desk and walked down the hallway. Along the way, he noticed how few people were milling about. In fact, the office was operating at maybe 40% staff. Quietly, Callahan PD had cleared out. David was clearly not the only one who had quit, not by a long shot. Isaac nodded at Johnson, who had stuck around. He was neck deep in paperwork.

"At least Johnson is still here," Isaac muttered. He entered the hallway and approached York's office. After pushing through a few journalists, he walked into York's office.

"Sit down," York invited.

Isaac shut the door behind him and sat in front of York.

York was, to put it simply, a mess. His ashtray was overflowing with cigarette butts and several prescription bottles of anxiety pills sat next to his paperwork. A few loose pills were scattered about. Isaac looked at all of it with nausea. He noticed a photo of York's wife, a pure southern belle, was discongruous in the clutter.

York took one last puff on the nub of a cigarette. He grabbed another from a pack on the table and lit it off the smoldering nub. He stuck the new one in between his teeth, adjusted his glasses and fixed Isaac with a level gaze.

"I'm promoting you to captain," he stated.

Isaac squinted in disapproval.

"Not Johnson? He's got rank."

"Isaac, you and I both know that... well... God bless him... Johnson is soft. You're not. You're... uh-" York couldn't think of a word.

Isaac snorted. "Well, Jesus, just call me an asshole, why don't ya?" he exclaimed.

York let out a dry chuckle. "Yeah, pretty much. Congrats. I'm losing men every day and at least I know you're not going to bail on me."

York took a long drag on his cigarette and blew the smoke out of his nose. "Now then, we're about to have a meeting with General Grey and you're coming with me. The meeting is going to be... bad. She's trying to implement Martial Law. Governor Randall gave her the green light when he instated her." York coughed and it didn't sound very healthy. He rubbed his bald head and took another drag.

"Get your shit together and meet me back here in ten," he said. "We'll head over then."

Isaac nodded. He started to get up but stopped and looked at York with concern.

"Anthony, are you okay?" he asked, sincerely.

York glared at his finished cigarette and stabbed it into the ashtray.

"No," he said and fished out another cigarette.

***

Isaac and York left Callahan PD and headed toward the National Guard offices.

"Grey's in one of these buildings," York muttered.

"What do you think of her?" Isaac asked.

"Cold and unfeeling - like you, but without the self-deprecating humor," York replied with a mild laugh.

"Damn, my one good trait," Isaac remarked wistfully.

"We can't let her turn this city into a prison overnight," York sighed. "So, we need to play this right."

Isaac shook his head. "Martial Law will destroy any chance Callahan has. It's her scorched earth tactic. What's holding her back from going through with it?"

York shrugged. "Oh, she wants to do it. I'm sure she revels at the thought of that much power. But she needs to have a solid reason, so the optics look good. She can either wait for another disaster like the hospital, or-"

"She can declare Callahan PD utterly ineffective, so military rule is the only option," Isaac finished.

"Now do you understand why I'm so stressed? We're hanging on by a thread. Every day that goes by without a tangible lead on the Ghost Killers...."

A uniformed soldier approached them. "This way, Chief York." He led them towards some makeshift barracks. The perimeter around the station essentially took up two parallel blocks of the city. National Guard was set up in various storefronts that had been "commandeered." The soldier took them past a row of tents, where several soldiers watched them with beady eyes. The soldier stepped inside a coffee shop and York and Isaac followed him.

"Chief York has arrived, ma'am," the soldier announced. General Grey had her back to the front door. Spread out on a table in front of her was a large map of the city, along with various intel. She was currently chewing out her chief of staff. Isaac and York waited while the poor man was grilled.

"Dismissed!" she finally ordered. He scurried out of the room, shooting Isaac a dirty look as he passed by. Meanwhile, Grey took a sip of black coffee and motioned for the two to sit down opposite her.

"I've brought Captain Murphy," York introduced. "He's one of the best detectives we have, and I concluded that he'd be perfect for the position."

Isaac looked over Grey and knew this conversation would go poorly. Grey's eyes flashed with anger and she snapped accusingly,

"You didn't think to consult me about your decision to promote him?"

Isaac started to snap back but York held up his hand.

"With all due respect, ma'am, it was my decision to make."

Grey's lips tightened and a vein on her temple throbbed. She held out her hand, and York placed Isaac's file in it. She flipped it open and scanned the resume wordlessly. After a moment she casually tossed the file to the side like a piece of garbage. Isaac's hand balled into a fist.

Grey set her sights on York with a disdainful expression.

"I pray that you have good news for me. What has Callahan PD found out about the Ghost Killers in the last week?" Her gaze bored into York's and he twitched his fingers, obviously wishing for a smoke, but that wasn't going to happen. He didn't answer.

Grey clicked her tongue. *Tut-tut!* She crossed her legs and locked her fingers together. "Every day, more men, women and children die. Every day, Callahan PD fails them. The fall of Callahan rests squarely on the shoulders of failures like you two. It's time for the kids to step aside so the grownups can take over. Martial law will go into effect tonight. Anthony, you are to report directly to me from now on. Dismissed."

Isaac smacked his hand down onto the coffee table, causing York to jump. The dozen or so soldiers, who were there for security, jumped as well. Grey shifted her gaze to Isaac with a small smile and raised eyebrows. Trembling with fury, Isaac met Grey's indifferent gaze and realized she regarded him as nothing more than a bug, a minor annoyance.

"You can't declare martial law. Callahan will be destroyed," he glowered. Grey smiled in faux compassion.

"The ends will justify the means," she declared. York held out a hand to hold Isaac back.

"Isaac, please," York pleaded, then turned to Grey. "General Grey, please consider the consequences that martial law could have on this city. This city is so close to falling over the edge, that an action like that would be the final straw. You can't do this. Please. I need more time. I swear to God, I will bring in the Ghost Killers."

Grey cracked a degenerate smile and her eyes widened.

"Swear to me," she ordered.

York was taken aback by her demand. He took a breath, gathered himself and nodded.

"I swear to you," he whispered, broken. Grey giggled and it was a putrid sound.

Isaac started to get up to leave.

"Martial law will still go into effect tonight," Grey declared.

York melted in his seat. "You... you're monster," he gasped.

Grey rose to her feet and stood over the humiliated York, who couldn't meet her gaze.

"That is correct. I can do whatever I want now. I have full control." Grey clicked her tongue and gestured to the soldiers. Grey took a sip of her coffee as the soldiers approached to escort Isaac and York out.

"I'm demoting you as well. There will be no chief for the time being. That job will fall under my jurisdiction. When the Ghost Killers are hung, you will be reinstated." Grey cocked her head and stared at York with a demonic gleam in her eyes.

"Though to be honest, it might be better if you died along with them. At least your name might retain a shred of dignity."

Isaac saw blood red. He wanted nothing more than to shoot a ragged hole into Grey's smiling face. His hand involuntarily moved to his holster and Grey sighed, unimpressed.

"Do you really think you could squeeze off a shot before my soldiers ventilated your skull?"

The cold muzzle of an M4 rifle jammed against the back of Isaac's head. *"Inhale. Count to five. Exhale. Count to five."*

Isaac took his hand off his holster. Grey took another sip of coffee.

"Detective Murphy, you have an impressive resume. Your work in the past has been nothing short of exceptional. It's a shame you've been rather lackluster as of late. It makes me wonder..." Isaac's heart began to pound as Grey leaned in right in front of his face. He stifled a gag.

"It makes me just wonder," she continued, "if you're such a great detective - such an excellent police officer...." Her eyes gleamed with faux compassion.

"How come you couldn't save your poor wife and daughter from being butchered?"

Isaac's face contorted into a morbid scowl as an inferno erupted inside of him. He leveled the flames at Grey with a burning stare and sneered,

"You think you're a monster, do you? Well, you're *nothing* in the face of a *true* monster. And when it finds you, it will tear you limb from limb."

Grey blinked.

Isaac stepped away without a further word, hoisting York to his feet and pulling him outside.

***

It was 8:00 p.m. when Isaac noticed the flash of red out of the corner of his eye. He turned his head to look out the living room window as several National Guard armored Humvees rolled by the quiet streets of his neighborhood. A loudspeaker blared the following warning,

"Martial law is now in effect. Martial law is now in effect. Curfew is in one hour. Martial law is now in effect…"

Isaac turned back to the television and flipped to the local news, which was explaining the rules of martial law. They said that anyone who was caught out after 9 p.m. would be arrested. Anyone who resisted would be shot.

"I'm sorry, Emily," Isaac whispered. He turned off the television and went up to the nursery.

***

The next morning, Isaac was struck by the silence as he walked into Callahan PD. He looked up the entrance hall and saw nothing. He focused on his hearing and didn't hear a peep. There was not a scratch of a pencil or a footstep. It was dead silent. The days when Callahan PD was as buzzing as a beehive were gone. Slowly, carefully, and as subtly as possible, people had left for good. Even the press had left. Too many journalists had wound up dead, many on camera.

Isaac passed the reception desk which sat empty. He remembered the friendly assistants who managed the desk and greeted everyone who came in.

Isaac walked to the forensics lab, where two specialists were staring at their computers. They were the only ones there. A faint smile crept onto Isaac's lips, because his friend Nathan was gone. True to his word, he'd quietly abandoned the sinking ship weeks ago.

Isaac crossed to the armory, where Officer Austin greeted him dourly.

"Eerie, isn't it?" he asked. Isaac nodded and moved along. He plodded up the steps and walked into the homicide department, which still had a semblance of business as usual. York and a few other detectives were going over a possible lead.

Grace was seated at her desk when Isaac sat down in his.

"Good morning, Isaac," Grace greeted him, without looking up from her work.

"Morning," he replied. "It's surreal, isn't it?"

"Well, at least it's quiet now," she muttered sarcastically.

Isaac pulled up Emily's case and re-examined the map of the city, before pointing towards the tunnel.

"We still have the tunnel. If 'Eight' is anywhere, that's our best option," Isaac stated.

"The tunnel is not going to happen, at least, not with just the two of us. We'd need an army to go in there. The stories I've heard.... it's a no-go zone," Grace warned.

"It's where Billy ran off too," Isaac muttered.

Grace rubbed her temples. "It's suicide. But I can help present the idea to the team later. Maybe they'll find a reason to pursue it. If the Ghost Killers are out there somewhere, they could be hiding in that tunnel."

Suddenly, the doors to the homicide department burst open, causing everyone to turn in surprise. It was Johnson. His face was doused in sweat and there was terror in his eyes. He stammered at York, "York! Dispatch just reported. Your house...."

York's eyes widened in absolute horror.

"Oh, Christ," he whispered. He dropped what he was holding, causing his coffee mug to smash, and took off at a dead sprint for the parking lot. Isaac grabbed Johnson's elbow and followed along with the other detectives. Isaac shouted back at them, "Stay put and do your jobs! I'll find out what's going on!" Everyone else stopped in their tracks.

Isaac continued after York, who was already jumping into a squad car. York turned on the siren and accelerated onto the street, almost running over a National Guard soldier. Isaac and Johnson jumped into another cruiser. Johnson hit the gas and peeled out after York. Isaac turned on the radio for dispatch and asked for the situation. The radio crackled and a disembodied voice reported, "Repeat, 713 at the residence. No additional backup requested." Dispatch went quiet.

Isaac swore loudly.

"A 713. Double homicide," he choked.

Johnson's glasses had fogged up from sweat. "His son's only three," he whispered, wiping his glasses quickly with a rag.

Isaac closed his eyes and saw the saw the surgeons cutting Emily's belly open. They reached into the cavity....

Johnson went as fast as he dared as they approached the bridge. The speedometer read 105 mph. York was going about 140. Just another minute....

Isaac gritted his teeth and steeled himself. *"Don't let it be like Emily. God, please..."*

They pulled up to the York residence. York was sprinting across the lawn, his squad car totaled against a tree behind him. His glasses had fallen off and he was sobbing uncontrollably. Several neighbors and the responding officers tried to stop him as he lunged for the front door.

"Ashley! Jonas! *I'm coming*!" he screamed. Johnson stopped the car and Isaac jumped out, running after York.

"Sir, please. Not like this. You don't want to see them like this," an officer was begging as he tried to hold York back, but York shoved him with adrenaline spiked strength and barreled for the door, bursting into the living room.

"*No!*" he moaned like a wounded animal.

Ashley and Jonas had been carved to pieces. It was impossible to tell where one ended and the other began.

York collapsed to his knees as Isaac reached him. Isaac wrapped his arms around him and pulled him from the room. "Anthony, please, don't look," he begged.

Isaac dragged York from the house and onto the front porch, where they both collapsed. Isaac dimly looked up at the stunned stares of the neighbors and officers. A group of EMTs pushed past them and into the house. They immediately gasped in shock at the nightmare inside.

York shakily got to his feet. He stepped off the porch and the crowd parted for him. Isaac's eyes widened in horror as York reached for his pistol.

"Anthony. Give me your gun," Isaac ordered.

York turned around to face everyone, but he didn't look at them. He was looking at something far beyond the horizon. Isaac rose to his feet and held out his hand.

"Anthony, please," he pleaded.

In a flash, the muzzle of York's Glock 17 was pressed underneath his chin. The neighbors gasped and ducked for cover. The officers stood dumbfounded.

Isaac took another step with his hand outstretched.

"I'm begging you."

A faint smile lifted the corners of York's mouth.

"It's in my hands now," he whispered.

Isaac lunged for the gun.

York pulled the trigger.

Isaac's face was sprayed with blood and brain matter. York pitched forward and fell into Isaac's outstretched arms.

BOBBIT ROCK

7. On My Shoulders

"You can only take so much, before you do something rash."

Callahan's morgues had overflowed long ago. The cemeteries were out of room. There just wasn't anywhere for the bodies to go. Even neighboring towns were being pushed to capacity due to the sheer scale of bodies. Now the York family was added to that glut.

Meanwhile, Callahan PD had effectively lost its sovereignty. With York dead and 70% of the staff vacated, dead, or MIA, there was no leadership or direction left. General Grey called a meeting with the remaining staff and informed them that she'd be running the show from here on out. She took pride in this fact.

"You happy now?" Isaac barked, "You wanted him dead. You told him to die."

Johnson looked down at his feet and Grace ground her teeth.

Grey just raised her coffee cup with a smug smile.

"Well, it certainly is more practical for all authority to be vested in me. Dismissed."

***

Isaac, Grace, and a few other detectives slumped, dejected, in their office. Outside, night had fallen, but the yells of the protestors were deafening. It was painfully apparent that these weren't simply protestors anymore. They weren't scared citizens or anxious civilians. They were anarchists. Callahan was breeding this type of denizen and martial law was the cause of it. Violent uprising was the only response to military takeover.

Johnson's phone rang and he raised it to his ear.

"Okay… good. We'll deal with it when we can." He hung up and surveyed the group.

"We're going to transport them to Greenville. It's a bit of drive, but at least there's room."

"And the funeral?" Grace asked.

Johnson shrugged.

"That was the 'we'll deal with it when we can' part," he said.

A siren rent the outside air as several armored vehicles passed by.

"Martial law is now in effect! Curfew begins in an hour. Clear the streets!"

The crowds thankfully began to disperse. Johnson went to his desk and pulled out a flask and a few shot glasses. He poured them and handed everyone a glass. He held up his drink with bloodshot eyes.

"To Chief York," he toasted.

"To Chief York," everyone echoed. Silently, they drained their glasses. The sirens continued to wail. Grace glanced at her watch and shuddered. "I think we should get going before curfew goes into effect."

A rattle of popping compressed air broke the gloom and everyone jumped.

"Let's hope the rubber bullets do the trick. We don't need another shooting." Johnson exclaimed. He moved to the window but couldn't see much in the dark.

"Are we still living in a free country?" he wondered.

"Grey's country," Isaac muttered.

Grace stood up. "I'm serious. We should all get home," she insisted.

One of the new detectives raised an eyebrow. "They're not going to arrest us. We're cops," he said. A rattle of real gunfire reverberated outside on the street. Screams from protestors immediately followed.

"I'm more afraid of being shot than arrested," Grace said gravely.

Isaac started to object, but realized she was correct. Hurriedly, everyone started packing up to leave. Isaac threw on his coat, but Grace reached out a hand for him.

"Isaac. Are you staying with anyone?" she asked.

Isaac gave her a blank stare.

"No," he answered.

Grace frowned. "You shouldn't be spending so much time alone. It's dangerous. Everyone needs friends close by."

"David and I spent plenty of nights together," Isaac said, scowling. "Now he's gone. This city is cursed."

Isaac turned his back on Grace and stormed out.

***

With the armored vehicles broadcasting their warnings and another protestor slain, the streets had emptied. Isaac checked his watch, twenty minutes before curfew. He hurried his pace. So long as the train was still running, he'd be fine. He cursed himself for leaving in such a huff, but his anger had gotten the better of him, thus denying a ride home from Grace. He whipped out his cellphone and shot a quick text off to David.

"You okay? How's Charleston?" he messaged. Several text messages above that one had gone unanswered. Isaac shook his head, trying to dispel a sense of dread from his mind.

He entered the metro station and sat on a bench. It was completely deserted and peaceful. The train was on time and would be arriving in just a minute. Isaac took a deep breath and tried to calm his racing thoughts.

"Isaac.…"

Isaac turned toward the train tunnel that lay off to the right side of the station, the tunnel that could be housing Eight. He stood up and squinted through the dark.

"Somebody say my name?" he called out. He strained his eyesight, trying to see anything in the pitch-black tunnel. The smallest twitch of movement captured his attention. He squinted until his eyes were nothing but slits.

"What is-" Isaac's breath caught in his throat. It was unmistakable. A familiar skeletal frame, ensconced in shadow, was dragging itself out of the tunnel.

Woosh! The train came hurtling by and blocked Isaac's view of the tunnel. In a daze, he climbed aboard and sat next to a window. He stared out the window at the tunnel but saw nothing. Unease knotted in his stomach as the train doors closed. He glanced around the empty cabin. Besides the conductor, he was completely alone.

Chac-Chac-Chac the train wheels creaked as the train picked up speed. The train made a turn. *Screech!* The sound was deafeningly loud. Isaac stuck his fingers in his ears because he legitimately felt pain.

"What the hell!" he swore. He stood up from the dirty plastic seat and gripped the handrail. The train entered the tunnel and the cabin became pitch black, aside from the strobing effect of passing lights. *Flash-Flash-Flash*

Chac-Chac-Chac Screech! Chac-Chac-Chac Screech!

Isaac shivered and moved a hand to his gun, unclasping the latch and resting his palm on the butt of the Glock. Something wasn't right here....

The train picked up more speed, absolutely hurtling down the tracks at a nauseating pace. It hit a turn and Isaac was thrown against the side of the cabin. He cried out in pain as he smacked into the window.

Chac-Chac-Chac Screech! Flash-Flash-Flash

The sound of the train was ear splitting. The strobe effect was seizure inducing. Isaac staggered to the front of the cabin, where the conductor's cabin was, and pounded on the door.

"What the hell is going on?!" he demanded. There was no answer. He squinted in the dark, unable to see through the window.

Flash-Flash-Flash

Isaac's jaw dropped. There was no one driving the train. He stumbled away from the door and accidentally toppled over a seat.

Screeeech!

The train picked up even more speed, and the outside view became an incomprehensible blur. Isaac drew his pistol and clambered onto a seat, fighting nausea from the vertigo inducing speed of the train, the splitting noise and strobing lights.

Wheeze....

Isaac's heart dropped to his stomach. He turned toward the back of the cabin, slowly, as if he were moving in cement. At last, he faced the back of the pitch-black cabin.

Flash-Flash-Flash

The Wretched Man laid crumpled on the metal floor. Isaac gasped in terror and all the blood left his face. With a shaking hand, he raised his pistol to the monster. But then the light cut out, drowning Isaac in darkness. He jumped to his feet in horror, unable to see where the Wretched Man was. He swept the muzzle of his gun blindly, through the darkness, trying to see something... anything.

Flash-Flash-Flash

The Wretched Man had closed half the distance to Isaac, oozing across the floor. The cabin was filled with the scraping sound of bone on metal and the cracks of stressed bones snapping. Isaac felt the strength begin to leave his limbs as a panic attack began. He choked and pulled the trigger.

Boom!

The gunshot reverberated off the confined metal walls of the cabin, literally deafening Isaac. The bullet slammed into the Wretched Man's face. Bone fragments flew from the wound, blood spurted, and flesh was ripped apart. But the Wretched Man did not stop. He continued, unabated, in his crawl toward Isaac.

Isaac, meanwhile, had collapsed to his knees, clutching his ringing ears in agony. The Wretched Man began to raise his head, to look Isaac in the face. Isaac tore his gaze away and raised his gun again as the darkness came back, plunging the cabin once more into darkness.

Blind and deaf, Isaac desperately tried to find the Wretched Man, feverishly pointing the gun left and right, unable to make out anything.

Flash-Flash-Flash

The Wretched Man was gone. Isaac swept the cabin with the muzzle of his pistol, but there was nothing. He shook his head and blinked. "*Where?*"

He smelled sulfur. Then he noticed it in his peripherals, something ashen in color. He glanced down at his chest. Two gnarled, toeless feet attached to skeletal legs hung down from his shoulders.

Isaac screamed bloody murder.

The train halted abruptly, sending Isaac flying. The doors opened and he scrambled to his feet and practically dove from the cabin. He staggered off the tracks, narrowly missing the electrified rail that would have electrocuted him. He stepped up on to the side of the tunnel and took off running towards the exit. Frantically, he checked his shoulders but didn't see anything. He wanted to turn around and look at the train but didn't have the courage to do so.

He set his head low and ran as fast as his legs would carry him. He passed by dozens of homeless people and anarchists who stared at him in surprise. He burst out of the tunnel and sprinted towards the road, barreling down the street like a madman, refusing to look back. He was committed to running as hard and fast as possible.

The exertion was exhausting. Isaac's lungs began to burn as he ran for his life; ran for his sanity. *"Can't slow down. Keep running. Keep Running!"*

Isaac's face flushed with effort. A moment later, he started gasping for breath. *"Faster!"*

Wheeze...

Isaac gave it his all, willing himself to keep sprinting. He had to outrun the devil.

Gasping for breath, he kept sprinting as his face turned red. The storefronts around him reflected him in their dark windows. There were dozens of reflections, each one showing another angle, another Isaac. Two dozen Isaacs ran for their lives. Isaac started to sputter, heaving for breath from his burning lungs. *"Can't stop now. He's right behind me!"*

He poured on the speed, sucking in air as his lungs caught on fire. His face had now turned purple. The corners of his vision began to close in. "Please! God!" He turned a corner.

"Emily!" he choked as his breath caught in his lungs.

She was standing in the middle of the road, cradling her large belly and looking at Isaac with those shining green eyes. Isaac reached out and took her hand.

"Come on, baby! Run!" he yelled. But Emily struggled to keep up, cradling her stomach awkwardly as she followed on shaking feet. Isaac looked back, aghast, sweat running down his face. "I got you, Em!" He picked her up in his arms, grunting at the weight on his tired legs. With a gasp of breath, he picked up the pace again with her in his arms.

"We're gonna make it! We're gonna-" Isaac gasped as he turned a corner. The walls of windows continued, and Isaac scanned them all, searching for the Wretched Man.

"I think he's gone!" Isaac skidded to a halt with a hammering heart. His arms were empty.

"Oh, Christ," he exclaimed. He whipped back and forth, looking for Emily, but the road was abandoned. A thousand Isaacs furiously searched for her.

"Emily!" he screamed. His voice echoed up and down the walls of mirrors.

A shiver ran up Isaac's back. Trembling, he turned around.

The Wretched Man was sitting on Emily's shoulders. Isaac drew his pistol and fired at the monster. The storefront window shattered. Isaac continued to fire at the reflections, howling in anguish. Glass exploded all around him and rained down onto the street as glittering dust. The refracting light made little rainbows and it was almost beautiful. Isaac collapsed to the asphalt, exhausted. He strained to get some air into his wrecked lungs, with his mouth and tongue as dry as sandpaper.

His Glock 21, still smoking, sat empty next to him. He coughed painfully and spat onto the ground. With shaking fingers, he reached for the pistol. Shoving a trembling hand into his jacket, he withdrew a fresh magazine and reloaded the pistol. He popped the slide of the pistol forward and shakily got to his feet. He gazed at the shattered windows and tried to regain his composure.

Suddenly, he was assaulted by a harsh yellow light. He squinted and held up a hand to shield his eyes from the intensity.

"What is that?" he asked. The light strengthened, casting a solid spotlight on him. The distant sound of a motor filled the air.

"What in the hell," Isaac whispered. He could barely see; the light was searing in the darkness. The motor grew louder until it couldn't have been more than fifty feet away.

A loudspeaker clicked on and a frantic voice boomed into the night, "Gun! Ghost Killer! Open fire!" Isaac's eyes grew wide. He dropped the Glock to the ground.

"N-No! Wait!" he stammered, raising his empty hands. A soldier in the armored vehicle raised an M249 light machine gun and trained the sights at Isaac's head. To Isaac's right was an alleyway. He had only a split-second to make a decision.

He dove for it. The soldier pulled the trigger.

Gratatatatatata! 5.56 rifle rounds lit up the street, windows shattered, doors were turned into swiss cheese and bullets ricocheted off the pavement.

A molten whip lashed Isaac across the cheek as he dove through the air. He hit the ground hard and clambered to his feet, sprinting for his life. Blood began streaming down his neck and onto his shirt. He stumbled further down the alleyway, looking for an escape. Behind him, two soldiers hopped off the armored vehicle and ran into the alleyway. They raised their MP5 submachine guns and sprayed the alleyway with automatic fire. Isaac reached the connecting street and dove again to avoid the onslaught of 9mm bullets, narrowly avoiding being cut to ribbons again. He staggered down the street, hearing the slap of heavy boots and spinning wheels behind him.

Running on pure adrenaline, Isaac didn't feel a thing. He hadn't even noticed he'd been shot. He tripped and smacked his chin on the pavement, busting the skin wide open. He clambered back to his feet and kept sprinting, but the rush of energy was about to expire. A wave of pain began to overtake him as he approached the literal end of the road. He heard more gunfire behind him and made one last push to the guard rail.

This was the end. There was nothing but the Palmetto River in front of him.

Isaac turned around, a bloody mess, and stared at the incoming armored vehicle. The two soldiers were opening fire again, and the ground was lighting up with ricocheting bullets. Isaac took a breath and jumped into the river. As he hung suspended in the air, he momentarily wished one of the bullets would find its target, and it would all be over.

Splash!

The current in the Palmetto River was well known to be vicious, and Isaac was immediately whisked away beneath the dark water. He floundered around in the water, trying to swim, but the current snatched him, and it was immediately an effort not to sink.

The soldiers reached the bank and fired into the water until the sergeant finally roared, "Cease fire!" As the smoke cleared, the soldiers scanned the river.

Isaac was gone.

***

For the first thirty seconds, it was all Isaac could do to just keep his head above water. He was a strong swimmer, but his strength was gone. He tried to keep a basic tread going, willing some energy to return to his arms. The water was cold, especially at night, and Isaac's teeth began to chatter. By some miracle, he spied a piece of flotsam and latched onto it. Holding on for dear life, he put his head down for some welcome rest. After some time, the current pushed him to shore. He clambered out of the water and collapsed to the ground, falling into unconsciousness.

When he came to, he tried to get a bearing on his location. He could tell he was in the outskirts of Callahan. He half crawled to the nearby road, noting the street sign, and pulled out his soaked phone. He gave it a shake and pressed the power button; it sprang to life, telling him it was 2 a.m. "*Thank God they're waterproof now.*"

He rang Grace, who picked up on the fourth ring.

"Isaac?" she asked, bleary from sleep. "What is it? What's going on?"

Isaac started to answer but was interrupted by a coughing fit. He collapsed to the grass and did not get back up.

"Are you okay?" Grace exclaimed, now wide awake.

"Grace... I've been shot... I need you... to-to pick me up and... hospital. I'm sending you... a... location." Isaac hastily texted Grace the street address.

"Dear, God! I'm on my way. Where were you shot?"

"On the cheek. Can you... stay on the line with me... until you get here?"

"Of course. Now, stay with me. Just focus on your breathing."

Out of the corner of his eye, Isaac saw his reflection in a puddle. The graze beneath his left eye dribbled crimson down his face in a macabre fashion. He closed his eyes and laid back on the grass.

***

The following afternoon, Isaac half dozed on his couch. His right cheek sported a fresh zipper of stitches, just underneath the eye. His chin was also bandaged up.

"That doctor was nice. Shame we had to go to the next county to get medical help." Grace said as she placed a bowl of hot chicken noodle soup in front of him. She sat in the recliner, with her own bowl, and watched him eat. She looked at his face and grimaced.

"This can't stand. You'll be scarred for life. It's a miracle you weren't killed. Grey is out of her mind. If the soldiers are cleared to shoot cops, they'll shoot anyone. We have to-"

Isaac cut her off without opening his eyes.

"There's not a damn thing we can do. It's her city now. Besides, I was out after curfew."

Grace scowled but Isaac managed to put on a meek smile.

"But I was able to get a good look at the tunnel. Eight could be down there. There's a lot of people down there."

***

The next morning, Isaac stepped out his front door and looked at his car - Emily's car. He pulled out the keys and unlocked it. He turned and looked off into the woods, where the Bobbit Rock stood miles away. He shook his head.

"Come on, Isaac," he whispered. He shakily touched the doorframe, gripping it tightly. He took a deep breath. "Inhale. Count to five. Exhale. Count to five. "

He sat on the driver's seat and put the key in the ignition. The car revved to life. He pulled out of his driveway and headed for the city. The sky was grey and somber. Any moment now, it would begin to cry.

As he neared the bridge, his phone rang - It was David. Startled, he answered the phone and pressed it against his ear.

"David!" he exclaimed. There was a long pause.

"Hey," David said quietly. The rain began and Isaac turned on the windshield wipers.

"Man, it is good to hear your voice. How's Charleston?"

On David's side, he was driving his motorcycle. It began to rain on him as he peeled off the interstate.

"I'm not in Charleston anymore. I just turned off for Callahan," David stated.

Isaac's eyebrows lowered.

"You're coming back to work?" he asked.

The rain picked up and David shuddered.

"Riding on a bike in the rain is misery. Raindrops sting you like bees, and it's so cold." David touched the throttle and settled at about 50 mph.

A knot formed in Isaac's stomach.

"David... what's wrong?" he pressed.

David sighed with empty, worn out eyes. He nudged the throttle again, throwing caution to the wind.

"You can only take so much, before you do something rash."

Isaac hit the brakes and pulled over onto the shoulder. A bead of cold sweat formed on his temple. He leaned forward in his seat, clutching the phone as tight as possible.

"David, what did you do?" he asked through gritted teeth.

David approached a red light and blew right through it. He glanced down at his gloved hands, and his gaze froze on the long blood stain trailing down his right thumb.

"I killed her... I killed them both," he breathed.

Isaac closed his eyes and took a slow breath. He exhaled and opened his eyes.

"Where are you?" he asked.

"Amy is so young; they would have raised her to hate me. They would have spun lies and stories about me being abusive and an alcoholic. Darling stepdad James had to rescue mommy from the bad man." David nudged the throttle again, approaching seventy in the rain. He barely dodged a large puddle that would have wrecked him.

"Where?" Isaac whispered.

David winced. "I went to his mansion on Shem Creek. I knew they were there. That's where she'd go on her 'business trips.' And I knew they had a babysitter for Amy so they could *have their alone time.*"

David blinked back tears and took a breath before continuing. "I knocked on the front door with my gun in my hand. James opened it and... I shot him right there, right between the eyes. And he just... dropped. No bullshit. No nothing. One minute there, then just... gone. Just like that. Then I went inside and-"

Tears started spilling out of David's eyes.

"She was begging for her life Isaac, pleading with me to spare her - spare her for Amy's sake."

David coughed and hit the throttle again.

"I killed her, then I left the gun, got on my bike and here I am. I'm going to drive to Callahan PD and turn myself in," he finished.

Isaac glanced up at the pounding rain that was pelting his windshield. He knew that David must have been driving blind.

"I had to do it. I couldn't let them take Amy from me. I love her so much..."

A tear ran down Isaac's face. He was heartbroken for his friend and heartbroken for the little girl.

"Promise you'll take care of her, Isaac. Promise me," David begged.

"I promise," Isaac whispered. David smiled ever so slightly.

"You'll be the father you were meant to be."

Isaac shook his head. "No. You will always be her father. Nothing will ever take that away from you. Nothing."

"You're my brother, Isaac. I love you."

There was a pause and all Isaac could hear was the distant roar of David's motorcycle as he hit 100 mph.

"She was there at the beach house," David whispered.

"The upside-down woman?" Isaac asked.

"She's not going to leave me, is she?" David asked.

Isaac bowed his head as David shot by him on the road toward the bridge. Isaac swallowed, trying to get rid of the lump in his throat.

"David, you've got to slow down," he choked out.

David shivered, again. He looked left. Clear. He looked right. Clear.

"It's okay," he whispered.

David looked up.

The upside-down woman was hanging above him.

David lost control and the motorcycle skidded on the rain-slick street. The bike flipped and David went airborne at 110 mph. He landed headfirst, his helmet crumpling against the unforgiving asphalt, before bouncing and skidding for several hundred feet. Isaac watched on in horror.

"David!!" he screamed. He burst out of the car and sprinted to his friend.

"Oh, God," Isaac moaned as he reached David. He fell to his knees in front of his best friend. David was a mangled mess. His legs were bent unnaturally and crushed beneath his torso. His left foot had been torn off and a piece of bone stuck out of his shin. His left arm was shattered in two and his neck was obviously broken. His eyes were still open, and the glassy orbs stared at Isaac, blankly. Isaac reached down and cradled David's body.

"Why? Haven't we suffered enough?" he sobbed.

When he could find the strength, Isaac pulled away from his best friend and shakily pulled out his phone. He dialed 911, but the line rung and rung. No one answered. Isaac looked at the road for help from a passerby, but it was completely abandoned. This was one of the busiest roads in Callahan, and not a soul was on it.

Just about the only people left in the city were the ones who wanted to destroy it. Isaac took David's hand.

"I can't leave you here. I'm gonna take you - take you... somewhere." Isaac groaned and lifted David onto his shoulder. A crack of bone accompanied the movement and Isaac bit his tongue. On trembling feet, he carried David back to his car and laid him gently in the backseat. He then shut David's eyes and closed the door. When he fell into the driver's seat, he dug out his phone and called Grace.

"Grace, David... he's dead. I'm taking him to the station. He... killed his wife." Isaac hung up, steeled himself and turned on the car.

***

Isaac drove slowly; it was all he could do to keep the car on the road in his current condition. He was on the precipice of a breakdown. The car reached the bridge and Isaac steadied himself. He felt an irrepressible urge to look back at David.

"Don't do it," he said to himself.

He blinked and tried to focus on the road. A lone car drove by in the opposite direction. Isaac made eye contact with the driver. He responded with an empty stare, another broken man.

"You killed me," David rasped to Isaac.

Isaac's heart froze. He tried to crank his neck to look at David but didn't have the courage. With trembling lips, he said, "I didn't kill you."

Flecks of blood dribbled from David's mouth. Though his eyes didn't open and his body didn't move, his tongue did.

"You killed us all. You killed Callahan."

Isaac squinted through his tears at the road.

"Please stop," he begged.

David's voice grew louder.

"You brought the Wretched Man to Callahan to kill us all."

Isaac bit his tongue so hard he drew blood. He needed to snap out of it.

"Emily loved you. And you failed her. Everywhere you go, people die."

David coughed and blood sprayed across the backseat.

"Why didn't you leave with your curse? Why did you stay and damn us all? I hate you!!"

***

Isaac reached the station. The protestors had become a howling army. He pushed through the barricades and skirted around the protesters until finally reaching the parking lot. Grace was waiting with several other detectives. Wordlessly, they carefully pulled David from the car and laid him on a white sheet. Isaac rested a hand on his best friend's forehead for one final goodbye.

"I should have come over that night you were so scared," he whispered into David's ear. "I shouldn't have left you alone. I failed you. I'm so sorry." Isaac broke down and Grace pulled him into her arms. The remaining detectives watched on with sunken hearts.

***

A few hours later, Isaac, Grace and Johnson sat together in the homicide department. The station was quiet, save for a few rung-out officers and some red-eyed detectives. There was no order and no direction for anyone. It was purgatory.

Johnson spoke into his phone, keeping an eye on Isaac, whose face was pale as milk.

"Yeah. Same place we took York. Thanks again." Johnson hung up the phone and took off his glasses to rub his eyes.

"David will be where Anthony and his family are. Charleston police found the victims' bodies as well. We'll figure out the rest later."

The shouts of protestors had risen to a thunderous volume. Johnson peeked out the window and his eyes grew wide in fear.

"This is not good," he said. "I don't know if the National Guard can hold them back."

Isaac didn't respond. Grace patted his shoulder reassuringly.

"Come on, buddy," she whispered.

A rattle of automatic gunfire split the air and Johnson swore. Screams of rage from the crowd immediately followed the cries of agony.

"Shit! I gotta go deal with that," Johnson swore. He hustled from the office, leaving Isaac and Grace by themselves.

Grace continued to try and comfort her broken friend.

"He was my brother," Isaac whispered.

"Yes, he was," Grace replied softly.

Isaac looked off in a thousand-yard stare.

"We're about the only ones left," he mumbled.

Grace considered his words. Another sudden volley of gunfire made her jump.

"Yes," she said fiercely. "But we can't just give up. We must persevere. So many are counting on us."

Isaac threw his hands up in the air.

"It's over. I failed Emily. I failed Samantha. I failed... David."

"I think they would be proud of you," Grace proclaimed.

Isaac was taken aback. "How?" he asked.

Grace's eyes lit up. "Because you've stuck it out this long. You've never given up, and I know you won't give up now," she declared.

An empty smile flashed across Isaac's face. It's all one can do in the face of defeat - smile.

"So optimistic. What did we do to deserve you?" Isaac chuckled. Then his expression darkened in fear. He looked left. Clear. He looked right. Clear. He looked up. Clear.

He then leaned forward with an air of certainty.

"There are no Ghost Killers. We just want them to exist."

Grace tried to interrupt. "That's not tru-"

Isaac stood up and swiped his desk, sending the mountain of papers flying.

"Look at the evidence!" he ranted. "There is none! We've got a genocide going on and we don't have a clue of who is causing it! Six months ago, the best detectives in the world were working here! And now they've all left, or they're dead!"

Isaac stormed over to the window and glanced at the pandemonium below. Several protestors had scaled the barrier and were attacking the National Guard with improvised weapons... and firearms. More gunfire erupted. It was about to explode.

"There are no substantial forensics," Isaac continued. "So, when a man turns up with no head, I guess he just cut it off himself? Or when forensics does come back with something it's from a random person and we can't connect any dots. What does the murderer say when we interrogate them? Why the 'Wretched Man made me do it!'"

Isaac pulled away from the window and wrung his hands in fury and frustration. The zipper under his cheek gleamed with sweat.

"The hospital!" he continued. "A hospital blows up, and the only evidence we got was from patients howling about the fucking Wretched Man!" Isaac kicked a desk, scattering more things and nearly hitting Grace in the face with a flying coffee mug.

"Isaac, please calm down." She touched his arm, making him pause for a moment. She looked him in the eyes and said, "This town may have gone mad, but we haven't. Someone *is* behind this."

Isaac snorted and sat down heavily under the window frame. He clasped his hands as if he were praying. Behind him, the skirmish worsened.

"Do you believe in the devil?" he asked seriously.

Grace didn't answer.

Isaac brought a palm to his forehead. "Well, I do. I believe the devil is alive. I believe he walks the earth with us. I believe he was cursed to never die but continue to age. So, his skin has rotted. His body is ashen meat and bone. His nails are long claws. His eyes…." Isaac trailed off.

Grace listened with her eyes tightly shut.

"His existence is pure agony. So, he latches on to someone - and stays attached for their whole life, making them spread misery and agony everywhere they go. And that way, when the devil has taken everything from that person, when he has destroyed their life and poisoned their mind; that person's agony is greater than his. Their suffering eclipses his and that brings the devil joy."

Grace's eyes fluttered open and for a moment, green stared into brown.

"I summoned the Wretched Man at the Bobbit Rock when I was kid," Isaac confessed. "He has been latched onto me my whole life. He waited until I would be at my most happy, the birth of my daughter, before taking her from me. Just before that, he began poisoning the city I loved. This is all my fault."

Grace looked up at the ceiling and said a prayer. Then she knelt next to Isaac and took his freezing hand into her own.

"The devil lives in all of us. We can follow his way and suffer, or we can live as God intended. Grief. Rage. Misfortune. Misery. Death. It will happen but we can't let it destroy us, otherwise, the devil has won." Grace released his hand.

"I believe in *you*," she emphasized.

For ten minutes, Grace and Isaac sat on the floor in silence. Grace prayed while Isaac's mind raced. At last, he rose to his feet and examined the scene at the window.

"This is not good," he said. The protestors were breaking through the barriers en masse, many had guns and were beginning to open fire on the National Guard, who were shooting back. In the midst of a gunfight, an explosion sent shrapnel everywhere and shook the whole police department. Smoke clouded the sky.

"We have to get out of here – now," Isaac stated. The slap of shoes in the hallway made him turn. Johnson came into the room with a torn shirt and a bleeding stab wound in his stomach. He'd lost his glasses, but his pistol was in his hand with the barrel still smoking. He dropped the empty magazine onto the floor and loaded in a fresh one. Grace's jaw dropped.

"Johnson! Are you okay?" she exclaimed.

Johnson pushed past Isaac and looked out the window.

He ground his teeth and turned away from the spectacle. "We've got to clear the building ASAP," he said. "They just blew up a section of the barrier and they're pouring through. Let's get to the armory and-"

A Molotov cocktail smashed through the window and engulfed Johnson in flames.

***

There was a second of stunned silence. No one moved, not even Johnson. Through the hungry flames, he locked eyes with Isaac.

"What?" he gasped through the fire.

The flames swirled up and the pain struck - broiling, searing, heart-stopping pain. Johnson shrieked and flailed wildly. Isaac and Grace desperately looked for something to smother the flames, but it was too late. Johnson's screams became moans and they could only watch, stunned, as Johnson collapsed into the maw of the inferno. Another Molotov cocktail smashed through a window across the office and now half the room was on fire. The ravenous flames billowed out like a flood, immolating everything in sight. The wooden desks, the ceiling, the carpeted floor, all of it went up in smoke.

Grace grabbed Isaac and shoved him towards the hallway.

"Run!" she screamed. They stumbled from the hallway in a daze, coughing as the smoke burned their lungs. Grace cast a glance back at the inferno for one last pitiful look at Johnson.

"Come on, Grace!" Isaac exclaimed. The two hurried downstairs, only to find the first floor was also in flames. Austin came barreling through the flames with his shoulder on fire. Isaac ripped off his coat and beat Austin's shoulder with it until the fire was extinguished.

"Thank you. We can't get out this way! We'll have to jump out a window on the second floor!" Austin yelled over the roar of the fire.

The three fled back upstairs with the flames licking at their feet. Grace pointed beyond the homicide department, which was now a fiery hell.

"Chief's office! It's still clear!"

They ran for the chief's office and pushed inside. Moving to the window behind the desk, they viewed the chaos below. The mob had completely overtaken the barricades and was now swarming the premises. The National Guard was hopelessly outnumbered, but these soldiers weren't going down without a fight. Automatic fire rung out and scores of anarchists dropped. Trying to keep more people from breaching what remained of the barricades, they launched tear gas that clouded the air. The unmistakable *woosh* of mortar fire could also be heard. The mob wielded everything from knives, to handguns, rifles and even pipe bombs. Isaac watched a man, clad in all black and wearing a gas mask, hurl a satchel at a squad of soldiers; it exploded in a hail of nails and bolts in all directions, shredding the soldiers.

The window suddenly shattered from a gunshot and Austin doubled up in pain, clutching his right ear. Isaac and Grace moved to help him.

"Are you okay?" Grace asked. Austin removed his hand, showing a bloody ear. He stared at the blood on his hand and shook his head.

"It's okay - I don't even feel it," he stammered in shock. Grace grabbed York's jacket from the back of the desk chair and pressed it against Austin's head.

"Keep pressure on it," she instructed. She glanced over the window frame and grimaced. The view from the window was ominous – they would have to jump directly into the mob.

"We can't go this way! It's suicide!" Austin yelled.

Isaac glanced back at the hallway; the fire had almost spread to the door. Black smoke was filling the room and it would soon be impossible to breathe.

"No choice. We jump and push our way through." Isaac drew his Springfield and Grace did the same. Austin gritted his teeth and raised his pistol.

"Okay," he affirmed, blood trickling down his cheek.

"We jump and run through," Isaac said. "Shoot anyone who tries to hurt you. Get off the street and keep moving for the bridge." Another mortar landed nearby, and the smoke made for good concealment. Isaac raised his pistol.

"This is it! I'll go first, then Grace, then Austin."

He stepped onto the window frame, took a deep breath and jumped. The world slowed down as he felt the weightless sense of falling.

"Oof!" he groaned as he hit the ground. He rolled onto his shoulder and rose to his feet. Thick smoke and noxious tear gas filled the air, making it hard to see and breathe. He looked up at the window.

"Grace! Now!" he yelled. Grace jumped and Isaac broke her fall. He helped her to her feet and then looked up at Austin. "Jump!"

Austin poised to jump, but the crack of a bullet split the air and he fell to the ground, blood spurting from his shoulder. Grace caught him awkwardly, breaking his fall. Isaac whipped around towards the gunshot. The gas mask-wearing protestor stood there with an AR-15 clutched in his hands, its barrel still smoking.

"Pig!" he shrieked and aimed for Grace. He never had the chance to pull the trigger because Isaac put two hollow points into his mouth. The gas mask split open and a gush of blood poured from the murderer's lips. He dropped flat onto his back, dead. Grace hadn't even raised her firearm.

The tear gas and smoke began to clear - Soon the mob would see them. Isaac turned to his friends.

"We have to run!" he ordered.

Grace shook her head, trying to tend to Austin's gunshot wound. Isaac crouched beside Austin.

"I'm going to carry you," Isaac said. He moved to lift him, but Austin held him off.

"No way. You guys go on without me. Carrying me will get us all killed."

Grace started to argue but Austin's mind was already made up.

"I'm going to play dead. It's all I can do. Now go! They're coming!" he said with determination, rubbing blood on his face as he did so.

"Good luck," Isaac stated and grabbed Grace by the wrist to pull her away from Austin.

"Nothing more we can do. Now let's go. Hold your breath until we get through the gas!" The two detectives sprinted forward into the street, shoving past anarchists.

"Don't stop, Grace! Keep moving!" Isaac yelled.

A burly man grabbed Grace's arm, wrenching her away from Isaac. He pressed a massive kitchen knife against her neck and started to slit her throat as she screamed.

"Fucking Pig Bitch!" he roared. Isaac shot him right between the eyes. The back of his scalp ripped off, spraying bone, hair and brain matter all over the anarchist next to him. She screamed as the burly man collapsed to the asphalt. She instinctively raised a nickel-plated revolver at Isaac. Isaac fired two shots. Her thumb tore off her hand and the revolver went with it. The second shot popped her right eye like a balloon.

Grace watched in horror, with her gun shaking violently in one hand as she touched the small cut on her throat that was almost fatal.

"Run!" Isaac hollered. They pushed through the crowd once more. Isaac glanced down at his badge. It was only a matter of time before they were spotted again amidst the pandemonium.

"Hey, those are cops! Get 'em!" A scruffy man yelled from next to Isaac. Isaac tried to fire, but he was tackled before he could squeeze the trigger. The man brought a fist crashing into Isaac's jaw, stunning him. He pulled out a switchblade and swiped at Isaac. Isaac caught the man's wrist and the two wrestled for the knife. Meanwhile, a woman with facial tattoos raised a baseball bat and swung at Grace, who screamed and fired a bullet into her gut. The tattooed woman howled in pain, dropping the bat. Before Grace could get her bearings, a mammoth of a man seized her in a bear hug from behind, lifting her off her feet and sending her pistol clattering away.

"Gotcha now!" he screeched with disturbing glee.

The *woosh* of a mortar filled the air and it exploded just feet away from them, disorienting everyone. Isaac closed his eyes as everyone got their bearings.

"The Wretched Man!"

Isaac opened his eyes and met the horrified stare of the knife-wielder, who was frozen in fear. Isaac ripped the knife from his hands and stabbed him in the center of the throat. He twisted the blade and ripped it out, causing a gush of blood and air. Isaac shoved the dying man off him and stood up, covered in blood. He was met by the terrified gazes of the surrounding mob – all staring at a space above Isaac's head.

The Wretched Man was sitting on Isaac's shoulders.

Everyone turned heel and ran for their lives, screaming in fear. Isaac extended his hand to Grace.

"Come on," he whispered. Grace took his hand, and the two sped away from the mob, which had parted like the Red Sea.

They ran toward the bridge. As they passed by the large windows of a storefront, Isaac saw his hellish reflection.

"I'm so sorry, Emily," he whispered.

8. Green Eyes

"The city is lost and so am I."

Isaac and Grace, exhausted, entered the Murphy home and shut the door. Grace locked it and glanced out the side window. Emergency vehicles from neighboring counties rushed by, sirens wailing. National Guard trucks roared by as well. The night air was filled with distant gunshots and explosions. A tear ran down Grace's face.

"It's all fallen apart," she choked.

Isaac fell to his knees, feeling the onset of a panic attack. Grace knelt by him in concern.

"Isaac!" she exclaimed. Isaac frantically grabbed her hands with his bloodstained fingers, shaking like a leaf.

"Please don't leave me alone," he begged.

Grace's eyes turned red. "I won't. I promise."

Isaac continued to shake. His hands and feet started to feel numb and the pins and needles ran down his limbs. He thrust a limp hand at his collar, trying to loosen it as sweat poured down. His chest constricted and he couldn't breathe.

"I can't... I can't – Oh, God!" Isaac stammered as the panic attack took over. His vision filled with the memory of his reflection earlier, a blood-stained Isaac with the Wretched Man on his shoulders. Then he watched the people he killed tonight die by his hand one at a time. Then he saw Emily with the Wretched Man on her shoulders.

Grace took Isaac's hands into hers.

"It's okay! It's okay!" she repeated, trying to calm him down.

Isaac was plummeting toward a nervous breakdown. He gasped for air, but his lungs felt like they were full of sand.

"Can't…. breathe," he said in a strangled voice. His head was swimming and his vision started to close in tight. Isaac's eyes rolled up and he passed out.

***

Isaac held Emily's hand in the ambulance as the paramedics worked desperately to stop the bleeding. She reached out and took his face between her hands. Their green eyes locked. Emily had been intubated, but her eyes said "*I love you.*"

A gurgle of blood rose in her throat, splattering red against the intubation tube. Emily's eyes lost focus.

"No pulse, she's flatlining!" the paramedic cautioned.

"Sir! Back away, please!"

Isaac moved from Emily's side, still staring into her glossed-over eyes.

The rest was a blur until they reached the operating room.

Isaac, shell shocked and dressed in scrubs, stood by the wall behind the operating table as the team worked furiously. Outside in the waiting room, half the homicide department sat waiting for the news, including David.

There was no saving Emily, but an emergency C-section might extract Samantha in time, but she had been without oxygen since Emily had died in the ambulance.

Isaac's whole body shook, the weight of Emily's death not fully registering in his brain. The surgeon took a scalpel and sliced

Emily's belly. He reached into her abdomen and continued to cut as the team assisted. His hands disappeared inside for a heart stopping moment. Then, Samantha's head came out. The team gently pulled her away.

She was blue and cold. Her eyes were closed, and she did not cry. Isaac pushed away from the wall and approached his daughter. The surgeon, stone faced, carefully placed Samantha into Isaac's arms as the wrecked team watched in silence. Isaac brought his angelic daughter into his breast as the tears fell.

"My beautiful little girl," he murmured. He kissed her on the forehead.

"I love you… so much."

Isaac howled a soul-crushing, animalistic cry of agony.

***

Grace took Isaac's face in between her hands, just like Emily did. Isaac opened his eyes, expecting to see Emily's green gaze, but instead he saw Grace's warm brown eyes.

"I'm here. I'm here," she hushed.

Isaac's chest was still burning.

"Breathe," she said.

Isaac's eyes started to roll up again. Grace squeezed his face gently and rubbed her hand across his forehead like a mother would do to a child.

"Stay with me, poor thing. Come on. Breathe, with me." She slowly inhaled and Isaac managed to force a small gasp.

"There you go. Now come on. Let's go a little bigger. Here, count with me."

Isaac remembered when Emily calmed him down in the closet so many years ago.

"Inhale. Count to five. Exhale. Count to five," Grace said calmly. Isaac hesitantly drew in air, nice and slow. Grace smiled. "There now. Hold it for five."

A helicopter flew overhead with sirens wailing, but Grace and Isaac were in their own world.

"Let it out," Grace said. Isaac exhaled. "Again. Count to five."

Isaac counted in his head. "*One. Two. Three. Four. Five.*"

"Breathe." Isaac took another breath in, shaking on the entry. The breathing exercise continued for several minutes, until the color gradually returned to Isaac's face.

Grace smiled warmly and withdrew her hands from Isaac's face. Isaac was touched by her compassion. He hadn't felt kindness like that in a long time.

"Thank you," he breathed.

"You're welcome," Grace said sweetly with a brilliant smile.

Isaac stared into her eyes and saw so much of Emily in them. "You'll make a wonderful mother one day," he promised. Grace beamed, touched.

***

Isaac stepped out of the shower and stared at himself, naked, in the mirror. The stitch zipper under his left eye glistened in the half light. The eye itself was bruised and swollen. He rubbed a hand over his unkempt beard. He hadn't shaved in over a month. His finger traced the bandage on his chin as he looked at his grey hair.

The last few months had aged him ten years. He sighed and turned on the sink, splashing water on his face.

***

Isaac recovered enough to cook some supper, and they ate it in the living room with the television on. All the local news stations were off air. They had either been abandoned, or swarmed. Instead, the national news was on, covering the fall of Callahan. The images of Callahan, burning, reflected in Isaac's eyes.

"The damage is catastrophic, and hundreds of casualties have been reported. Much of downtown Callahan is in flames from arson and the mob is attacking without provocation. If you are in the city-"

Grace turned the volume down and took a bite of the chicken and green beans Isaac had made. She raised her eyebrows in surprise, "Isaac. You are a really good cook," she mused.

Isaac shrugged. "Ordinarily, I include a shallot and jam sauce for the glaze, but I haven't been able to go to the store recently for obvious reasons."

As if on cue, the power cut out and the lights and television went black.

"Damn," they said in unison, then shared a chuckle.

Isaac rummaged through a nearby drawer for a flashlight and candles.

"Well, going back to the city is suicide. So, we'll just hunker down and let the National Guard deal with the mob. A week from now we can pick up the pieces." Isaac struck a match and lit a candle, illuminating his face in a flickering glow.

"Perhaps it's best if Callahan burns," he added, ominously.

"I'm afraid it will... I'm sorry, Isaac."

"I promised I'd save Callahan. Now I've seen that that's impossible."

"A city is just concrete and asphalt. It's the *people* inside that matter. You can still save the people of Callahan," Grace encouraged.

Isaac clicked on a flashlight.

"Who's left that matters besides you and me?" he asked.

He handed Grace a spare flashlight and some batteries. They walked upstairs and Grace saw the open door to the nursery. Her eyes lit up.

"Amy," she proclaimed.

Isaac closed his eyes. "Amy's with child services now," he reminded her.

"David and Charlotte named you as her legal guardian if they were to pass away." Grace pointed out. Isaac chuckled darkly. He spread his arms wide and spat back at her.

"Look at me. Do I look like a capable father? I couldn't save my own wife and daughter. I couldn't save David. I'm racked with panic attacks. I think the Wretched Man has cursed me. I killed several people today. They weren't the first and...."

Isaac's eyes glowed darkly. He raised up his hands and looked at his palms.

"I'm afraid, because I don't think I felt anything this time," he confessed.

"The city is lost and so am I. I am a wretched-"

Grace hugged him tightly. Isaac jerked in surprise, but then slowly wrapped his arms around her.

"We'll get through this together," she vowed.

***

In the guest-bedroom, Isaac and Grace made-up the bed.

"Sorry about it not being made. It hasn't been slept in since…." Isaac winced.

Grace grimaced at the reminder of their friend. She looked out the window, where the sky had turned red from the fall of Callahan. Gunshots rang out in the distance.

"Do you think the mob will cross the bridge?" Grace asked, changing the subject.

"Very unlikely. They're going to focus on the National Guard. Plus, it's not like there's many people left on the residential side. The mob wants blood, so they will go where the people are."

Isaac led Grace out of the guest-bedroom and to the open gun safe in his bedroom.

"Just in case they do come here, there's a bunch of guns in there. But it's not just the mob that I worry about." Isaac's expression darkened and he walked to his bed, picking up the portrait of Emily, which he looked upon sadly.

"Are you okay?" Grace asked.

The vein on Isaac's temple throbbed as he tensed up.

"The Ghost Killers have to be real. If they're not, the Wretched Man is. And no one will be able to deny it."

Isaac touched the wedding ring on his finger as he looked upon Emily's face.

"I just wish she was here," he mumbled. Grace didn't know what to say.

A shadow passed across her face and she shivered.

"Do you think the woman I shot died?" she asked, trembling.

Isaac closed his eyes and recalled the tattooed woman doubling over in pain, clutching her bleeding stomach as her eyes bugged out.

"I don't know," he said flatly.

Grace's eyes welled up and Isaac hugged her for support.

"It'll be okay," Isaac whispered.

Grace nodded and broke apart from him. She gathered herself, before walking back to the guest-bedroom. She cast a wayward glance at the dim flashlight on the bed, which was the only source of light for the room. Dark shadows were everywhere.

"Should I keep the flashlight on? Just in case?" she asked.

Isaac cracked a dark smile and reached for the switch.

"No. Light won't help."

He flipped the switch.

Darkness.

***

Emily was lounging in the recliner watching television. She was only a few days away and her belly was quite large and distended. She gazed at it sweetly and gently placed her fingers on the bulge.

Outside, a heavy rainstorm was dumping buckets. After a moment, she felt her tummy rumble.

"Need ice cream." She got up, waddled into the kitchen and popped open the freezer.

"Where is that mint chocolate chip?" she muttered, searching for the container.

"Found ya!" She pulled it out and got a spoon from the drawer. As she returned to the recliner, her phone buzzed. She pulled it out quickly.

"Hey, honey! Forget something?" she asked.

"Yeah, I left my notes on the Larson case," Isaac said. He glanced in his rearview mirror at the bridge. "Should only be a couple minutes away. Maybe, I should just stay when I get home."

Emily shook her head.

"Absolutely not, the city needs you to be working. Don't worry about me, when the time comes, you'll be the first person I'll call," she insisted.

Isaac nodded, knowing she was right.

"Well, how are my two favorite girls doing?" Isaac asked.

Emily smiled. "Well, she's been demanding ice cream. Can't get enough."

Behind Emily, a dark shadow passed the living-room window. Emily dunked her spoon into the container and lifted the ice cream to her lips.

"Want me to stop for more?" he asked with a laugh.

Emily shook her head. "No please, don't! If I keep eating like this, I'll never lose the baby weight." Emily put down the spoon as Isaac sniggered.

"You're beautiful, sweetheart," he said, warmly.

"Yeah, yeah," Emily groaned, rolling her eyes.

The dark shadow moved to the front door. Knuckles rapped on the wood, causing Emily to turn in surprise. "Someone's at the door. In this rain?" she wondered.

Isaac's eyebrows narrowed.

"Can you see who it is?" he asked.

Emily took a step towards the door and looked through the peep-hole at the man. Ice blue eyes stared back at her. A wicked scar also ran across his left eyebrow, but the rest of his face was obscured by a black bandana and a cap. His figure was burly and imposing, pushing 6-6.

The man put his foot into the door, and it shook violently on his hinges. *Boom!*

"Oh, my God!!" Emily yelped. "He's trying to break in!"

Isaac immediately floored it, flipping on the sirens as he did so.

"Emily! Lock yourself upstairs and get the guns!" he instructed.

"No time!" Emily screamed. She scrambled to the dining table and hid underneath it. She held her breath as the man brought his foot back again. *Boom!*

The front door broke off its hinges, slamming violently against the living room floor.

"I love you," Emily whispered before holding her breath.

Isaac was going top speed. He hissed as quietly as he could.

"I'm thirty seconds away. I'm coming. I love you," he said. He flipped on the radio and called in the situation to dispatch.

"Officers are on the way, Detective Murphy," dispatch responded.

The man seemed casual and relaxed as he passed the threshold and peered around.

"Where are you hiding, little girl?" he questioned in an emotionless monotone.

Emily watched his tree trunk legs walk around the living room from underneath the table. His huge figure cast a massive shadow. His feet turned to the table.

"Now that's just pathetic," he mused, then rushed forward. Emily screamed.

"Emily!" Isaac roared into the phone. The house was in sight.

The man grabbed the dining room table and wrenched it away effortlessly with one hand. Emily rushed for the stairs desperately, but he immediately stabbed a shining knife into her thigh. Emily gasped, her heart catching in her throat at the horrendous pain. She fell to her knees as the vicious man loomed over her.

"Please..." she begged as he looked on, almost bored. He grabbed her by the hair and lifted her up. Emily shielded her belly with her arms. He slashed her across the cheek, cutting off her left ear in the process. He stepped back to admire his macabre handiwork, giving Emily the opportunity to dash for the stairs as blood gushed from her thigh and face.

The man reached for her ankle, but his fingers slipped on the blood. Emily reached the stairs on all fours and tried to crawl up them. At the same time, Isaac finally reached the house and slammed the brakes before jumping right out of his car, Glock 21 in hand. His car fishtailed in the rain and slammed into a tree.

"Hang on, Emily!" he roared.

The man drove the knife into Emily's leg again and a spurt of blood splashed across his bandana. He touched the blood and then reached a finger underneath his bandana to taste it.

"No, no, no. God, please!" Emily cried as he raised the knife again. Emily again shielded her belly with her arm. He plunged the eight-inch knife through her forearm and into her navel. Emily howled in agony and a stream of blood ran down the corner of her mouth. He pulled the knife back for a final blow.

Crack!" The knife clattered to the floor and the man stared, in awe, at his right hand, which now only had three fingers, turning him into the monster known as Eight. The bullet continued into the hallway wall, leaving a small hole. Isaac unloaded on Eight, putting twelve rounds into his chest.

Eight took off running for the living room window. One round missed his chest and tagged him in the shoulder. The rests of the bullets were ineffective, because he was wearing body armor. Realizing this, Isaac aimed at his head and fired again as he smashed through the window. The bullet missed high, scoring the top of Eight's scalp and ripping off a small chunk of flesh from his forehead along with the cap. He hit the ground hard and his bandana fell off. As he got to his feet, he looked up at Isaac.

Eight's face was scarred and disgusting. His mouth, grimacing in pain, sported grey and yellow teeth. His nose, bent and twisted, had clearly been broken many times. Short blonde hair covered his scalp.

Isaac leveled his sights at Eight's forehead and pulled the trigger. *Click!* Empty. Eight turned heel and disappeared into the pouring rain.

Isaac turned to Emily and fell to his knees, heartbroken.

"Oh, my baby," he moaned through tears. A knot filled his throat. Sirens wailed and tires skidded as responding officers rushed the house with guns drawn, but Isaac didn't hear them. Emily was his world.

He reached out and took Emily into his arms. She looked at him with sorrowful eyes as she held her hands over her bleeding stomach. Isaac pressed down on the stab wound, his hand over hers.

Emily's lips moved and she struggled to whisper,

"Please... sa-save Samantha."

"Emily," he choked out.

Emily stared deep into Isaac's eyes. "Save Callahan."

Her eyes began to roll up. Isaac gripped her tightly.

"I will... Please don't go! No! Please, God, don't go!" Officers entered the house and called for paramedics.

"No, please don't go. Please don't go, Em. Stay with me. Don't leave me," Isaac sobbed.

***

Isaac's green eyes flew open in the darkness. He sat up in bed, bathed in sweat. He let out a shaky breath and held his head in despair. *"How many times have I had this dream?"*

He glanced over at the portrait of Emily. He took another breath and tried to calm down.

Wheeze....

Isaac bolted upright in fright. He squinted at the large bedroom window opposite the bed. The brightness of the full moon outside shone dimly through its cloth shade. Isaac squinted as hard as possible but couldn't see anything else through the shade.

He heard it again.

Wheeze....

The Wretched Man appeared behind the window, pressing his skeletal frame against the glass. Isaac could only see his silhouette through the obscuring shade. The Wretched Man's foot-long talons of nails clicked against the glass as he leveled his corrupted gaze upon Isaac. Isaac screamed.

Crash!

The Wretched Man shattered the window and flew into the room. The sight of his nightmarish body rushing through the air was unspeakable. He slammed into Isaac, shoving him against the bed frame. The Wretched Man's oozing, bony fingers squeezed Isaac's windpipe, crushing the life out of him. Isaac's eyes grew wide as his face turned red. His vision constricted as death approached.

A woman's gasp startled Isaac. As his vision restored, he saw Grace's eyes bulging as he clamped down on her neck with his fingers. Her eyes rolled into the back of her head.

"Oh!" Isaac exclaimed and yanked his hands away from Grace, mortified at what he had done.

Grace gasped and began choking and coughing. As she sputtered for air, Isaac stared at his palms in horror.

"I didn't, mean to." Isaac stepped away from the reeling Grace. "What have I done?" he asked.

He rushed out of the room as Grace reached for him in vain.

"Isaac, don't - co-come back." She tried to restrain a hacking fit as Isaac ran down the stairs and out the front door.

Grace tried to follow him, but her weak knees buckled. "Don't be afraid," she whispered before passing out.

***

Isaac drove toward the city at top speed, ranting and raving to himself.

"It's my fault! I was cursed the day I raised him up!" he screamed, casting his gaze in the direction of the Bobbit Rock.

"The day I climbed that fucking rock! I brought him to this city. All of this is my fault! I am responsible!!"

In front of him, Callahan burned. Buildings had been fire-bombed throughout the night and the National Guard was actively firing on the violent mob at every turn. Isaac sped by a burning fire engine as anarchists and protestors heaved Molotov cocktails into storefronts.

"I'm a failure, Emily. I deserve this," he stated grimly.

The road in front of him was blocked by a burnt-out armored vehicle. Isaac abandoned the car and headed further into the city on foot. Bodies, both military and civilian, were strewn all over the streets. Gunfire echoed in every direction and the constant drone of helicopters buzzed in the sky. It was a living hell.

Moments later, Isaac entered the fray of an active shootout, but no one noticed him. He was a ghost in the war zone. Anarchists sprinted past him and bullets whizzed left and right, but he went by unscathed. Who cared about some muttering, half-naked, nutjob on the streets of Callahan?

A pickup truck rushed past Isaac. Attached to the trailer hitch was a long rope. At the end of the rope was a soldier. She was being dragged, facedown, along the asphalt at 60 mph. It hit a bump and the woman popped up into the air. Isaac recognized the uniform and distinctive haircut. It was General Grey. There wasn't any skin left on her face. Isaac kept walking.

***

Callahan Grand Cemetery was in sight. A burning Humvee sat in front of the gate as a lone soldier desperately tried to hold back the mob amidst his fallen comrades. He emptied the magazine of his M4 rifle, and several people dropped. He grabbed his radio and shouted into it.

"Backup! I need backup!" he pleaded. His throat suddenly split open from a 12-gauge shotgun blast. The mob began looting the Humvee and dead soldiers. Isaac ignored the carnage and walked into the cemetery.

"You were the only good thing that ever happened to me. And because of me, you died." Isaac whispered as he reached Emily's tombstone. His knees buckled and he fell to the dirt. "I wasn't good enough to save you. I wasn't strong enough, to not fear the Wretched Man." Isaac shoved his hands into the dirt.

"But I'll never let you go." He pulled his hands out and flung the dirt into the air. "I can't stand being away from you for one more second."

Isaac continued digging, tearing his fingernails off in the frenzy.

Outside the cemetery, backup had arrived for the dead soldiers. A half dozen Humvees rolled up, and machine guns appeared at every window. No order was given - the soldiers just opened fire. An ocean of bullets crashed into the mob, ripping them limb from limb, creating a red mist of blood. A few managed to return fire, but it was irrelevant. When the cease-fire was given, the soldiers hit the ground and began arresting the survivors.

Meanwhile, Isaac sat in the trench he had dug, his hands blistered and bleeding as he continued to lift earth from Emily and Samantha's grave. Behind him, a hulking figure approached.

"Isaac." It was Eight.

Isaac turned his head and stood up. He stared at the shining knife in Eight's left hand, the same knife that killed Emily. Eight pointed at the grave with his crippled hand.

"I was hoping to dig her up and fuck her. It looks like you've already done half the job for me."

An inferno conflagrated in Isaac's eyes.

"I'll kill you!" he roared in animalistic fury. Eight swiped at Isaac, who sidestepped and leaped on him, digging both thumbs into Eight's eye sockets. Eight screamed and stabbed Isaac in the side. Isaac pulled back, as the pain from the stab wound registered. Blood oozed from it, staining the ground of the dead.

Eight lurched forward and slashed at Isaac's face. Isaac ducked and grabbed Eight's arm. The two wrestled for the blade. It was a losing battle for Isaac because Eight was a massive man. Eight regained control of the blade. In response, Isaac bit Eight in the face, crushing his ugly nose between his teeth. With a *rip*, Isaac bit off part of it. Blood spilled out of the mangled appendage as Eight screamed in agony.

Isaac then wrenched the knife from Eight's wavering grip. He shoved the blade into Eight's hip and twisted it against the pelvis bone. Eight slammed his fist into Isaac's gut, sending him toppling into a tombstone. Eight grabbed a rock and brought it down toward Isaac's face. Isaac held up the knife and partially deflected the strike, so it bashed into his shoulder. *Crunch!*

With his good arm, Isaac slashed at Eight's ankle, severing a tendon and dropping him to his knees. Eight gasped and tried to return to his feet. Isaac jumped up and slammed the blade into the small of Eight's back up to the hilt. Eight again fell to his knees, this time permanently. Isaac twisted the knife and then ripped it out, before plunging it into Eight's collarbone. Isaac yanked on the handle, knocking Eight flat on his back. Eight held up a feeble hand to protect himself as Isaac sat on top of him. Isaac sank the blade directly into Eight's crippled hand, severing more fingers, before stabbing viciously into Eight's chest.

Once a knife starts stabbing, it's only natural to continue.

Isaac brought the knife into Eight's stomach, his face, his forehead, his heart, his groin, his throat. Down the crimson blade went. Over and over. Stab. Stab. Stab.

"Save Callahan," Emily's voice whispered in his ears.

Isaac jammed the knife into Eight's sinus and a torrent of blood gushed out. Exhausted and bleeding, Isaac fell onto the grave, still clutching the knife.

Meanwhile, the soldiers were still cuffing survivors and tossing them into transport vehicles.

It became evident to Isaac that he was *alone.* His eyes widened and he sat up. There was no blood. There were no wounds. There was no Eight. It was just Isaac, sitting on his wife's grave. A crazed smile grew on his face and he began to laugh. The laugh became a cackle, like a witch.

Isaac's wretched laugh echoed through the cemetery, alerting several soldiers to his presence. They approached him. One of the soldiers raised the butt of his rifle and cracked it across Isaac's skull.

***

Grace regained consciousness and weakly rose to her feet. She looked at herself in the bedroom mirror. Her neck was black and blue, and her throat was sore. The morning sun glinted through the window and she opened the shades. The fires of Callahan had been extinguished. In the opposite direction, the Bobbit Rock stood amidst the forest.

She turned and walked to the master bedroom.

"Isaac?" she called out faintly. She entered the empty bedroom and saw the open closet door. The hairs on the back of her neck stood up and she felt compelled to enter the closet. Without a thought, her feet carried her inside. The open gun safe stood waiting. Grace knelt and looked inside. Amongst the guns was a Bible. Oddly, there was a belt beside it, but the pages fluttered loosely. Wordlessly, she pulled it out. A sheaf of sketch paper was wedged between the pages. Grace fished it out and looked at it.

The finished drawing of the Wretched Man's face stared back at her. In his once-empty eye sockets were Isaac's green eyes.

BOBBIT ROCK

9. Bobbit Rock

*"You can live your life with the devil on your back and
be destroyed. Or you can look him in the eyes and tell him
that you are not afraid."*

Several months later, Isaac awoke from a deep sleep. He sat up on
his creaky cot and glanced around the institutional walls of his
cell in the Tubman Psychiatric Hospital. He stroked his large grey
beard and sighed. *"Inhale. Count to five. Exhale. Count to five."*

Isaac stood up and used the toilet before moving in front of
the sink. Isaac washed his face, brushed his teeth and drank some
water. Lastly, he gazed at himself in the shatter proof mirror. At
37, he was fully grey. Someone who didn't know him might think
he was nearly twice that age. His gaunt frame was skinny as a rail.
He could count every single one of his ribs. His appetite had been
nonexistent since the fall of Callahan.

He walked to a drawer and slipped on a worn jumpsuit along
with a pair of flimsy shoes. He then sat on his bed and clasped his
hands, trying to think of words for a prayer, but nothing came.

"Never was very creative," he whispered.

A loud buzz reverberated through the hallway and the rooms
on his ward. Isaac reluctantly stood up and approached the door.
It slid open automatically and he stepped out for the morning roll
call.

"Murphy!" an officer barked.

"Yes, sir," he acknowledged.

Isaac glanced over to his left. His neighbor had not appeared from his cell. The officer scowled.

"Get out here, Roberts!" he demanded. There was no response. The officer gestured to several other guards and they entered the room. Immediately the terrified squealing of the patient pierced the air. Isaac looked at his feet as the guards carried the frantic man out.

"No! Don't take my brain!! The Wretched Man!"

One of the guards jammed a syringe into the patient's thigh and he started to go limp. Isaac shook his head in disgust.

***

In the cafeteria, Isaac sat alone. The demented and disturbed ate voraciously around him. He nibbled on a piece of rubbery egg, immediately feeling nauseous. Unable to swallow it, he spit it out. He glanced at a woman who was in a similar situation. A Callahan survivor as well, her case was nearly identical to his. In fact, many patients had similar conditions. The cafeteria was packed with these poor souls - good people who had lost their minds from the 'Callahan Event.' Many were past the point of no return, but some, like Isaac, were clinging to sanity.

***

Weeks later, Isaac shaved off his beard, under the watch of a guard. He grabbed a trimmer and ran it through his hair several times, roughly cutting it into something more professional. After he was done, he looked much younger, aside from the dark bags under his eyes and stress lines. He finished and nodded to the guard. Today was the big day.

***

An hour later, Isaac sat in the visitor's center with several other patients all under the watch of armed guards. The entrance door opened, and Grace walked in. She was dressed smartly, in a blouse and blazer. She smiled at Isaac and his eyes lit up. She took a seat next to him and held out her hands. Isaac took them, thankful for the warmth.

"The lack of physical touch here is probably the worst part. It feels like I'm a ghost," Isaac said. "Thank you for coming. I'd be lying if I said I wasn't nervous."

Grace gave Isaac's hands another squeeze before pulling away. "You'll do a great job. Soon you'll be out of here," she promised.

"Thank you, Grace. If it weren't for you, I wouldn't even have this chance," he said sincerely.

Grace waved him off. "You know, it wasn't just me. There's been mounting public pressure for Governor Randall and the state house to pass this measure. Mental hospitals, prisons, every facility is overflowing with people who shouldn't be there. Not to mention the burden on the taxpayers to foot the bill for all the patients. They deserve the chance to prove their sanity and be let out with expunged records."

Isaac's eyes glowed warmly. "But you were the one who started the petition. Without you, who knows?"

"Austin says he's rooting for you, too," she remarked.

Isaac cracked a thin smile.

"I still can't believe he survived. Playing possum is underrated."

Grace started to respond, but Isaac's shoulders suddenly sagged. "What's wrong?" she asked.

Isaac exhaled slowly and nervously twitched his fingers. "They're not going to let me out because I still believe in him. That hasn't changed. I'm still in fear. I can't go in there and lie."

Grace leaned back in her chair and gave him a thorough once-over. He was a far cry from the mentor she met months ago.

"Can I ask you a question?"

"Of course," Grace replied.

"The night we were caught in the mob, the Wretched Man appeared on my shoulders after the mortar. That's how we escaped. The mob saw him and were terrified. You were right there - you had to have seen him. And yet, you've never mentioned it."

Grace didn't respond. Her eyes were lucid and focused.

Isaac leaned forward and said more fiercely,

"You *must* have seen him. You can't deny it."

Grace's eyes met Isaac's grim stare without hesitation. She took a slow breath in and said with absolute clarity.

"You can live your life with the devil on your back and be destroyed. Or you can look him in the eyes and tell him that you are not afraid."

A buzzer sounded and a guard stepped forward.

"Time's up. Let's go."

Isaac rose and the guard took him away. Grace gave him a reassuring smile when he looked back.

***

In the Evaluation Room, Isaac sat in front of a board of doctors. Dr. Brady sat next to him. Two bored security guards stood in the corner of the room as well.

Dr. Vincent Erich, the lead physician, leaned forward. He was in his seventies and had a well-groomed grey beard and black-framed glasses. He shuffled Isaac's file and scanned over the contents. Finally, he looked at Isaac and began.

"Good afternoon, Mr. Murphy. As you are aware, Governor Randall signed a bill a few weeks ago allowing the release and record expungement of anyone who fell under the Callahan Event so long as they received an acceptable evaluation. Upon Dr. Brady's repeated recommendations, we have decided to see you today for that evaluation. If you pass, you will be released."

Dr. Erich flipped to the beginning of Isaac's file. Isaac winced and glanced at Dr. Brady, who was stoic. Dr. Erich sighed as he read the contents.

"You were in quite a poor state when you arrived here. Psychosis, severe paranoia and routine outbursts. We were initially considering more... *drastic*... treatments."

Dr. Brady cleared his throat loudly. Dr. Erich glanced at him with disdain.

"Yes... yes... many of our Callahan patients arrived in similar states. This event of mass hysteria will surely be studied for centuries to come. But regardless, once we found the right course of treatment, your recovery was remarkable."

Isaac shivered at the word *treatment.*

Dr. Erich turned to several test scores.

"In the last few months, you've passed cognition tests with flying colors. You've been consistent with your medication consumption and have generally been an exemplary patient. That is commendable." Dr. Erich cleared his throat and adjusted his glasses. "And yet you remain unwavering in your belief of the Wretched Man. You still steadfastly affirm that you are 'cursed' by him. So, I ask you today - do you still uphold these convictions?"

Isaac cast a solemn gaze at the board members, before coming to a rest on Dr. Erich.

"Do you believe in God, Dr. Erich?" he asked. One of the doctors chuckled.

Dr. Erich did not look up from Isaac's file as he bluntly responded, "God is a figment of the foolish man's imagination. It is the primitive's way to explain that which he does not understand or would rather *not* understand. Believing in God is a way to wrap a blanket of ignorance over oneself. By doing so, one does not have to face the harsh reality of our existence. We are alone. We are mortal. And when we die, there will be nothing. There is no God, Mr. Murphy." Dr. Erich clicked his pen and scribbled a note. Satisfied, he peered at Isaac over the frame of his glasses. "However, there is life. And I do all I can to make that worth living."

Isaac glanced at Dr. Brady, knowing he wore a crucifix hidden beneath his white coat and tie.

"Dr. Brady is a proud Roman Catholic. Would you consider him to be *primitive?*"

A few board members shifted uneasily in their chairs. One of them snickered and cast a sidelong glance at Dr. Erich.

A small arrogant smile formed on Dr. Erich's lips as he shot another scornful look at Dr. Brady.

"Don't tempt me, Mr. Murphy. As much as I would relish the opportunity to agree with that statement-"

Dr. Brady interrupted with a dry guffaw in response. Dr. Erich waved him off.

"Very well, Dr. Brady and others like him are free to believe in God if they wish."

Isaac flexed his fingers, knowing he'd caught Dr. Erich. "Then what is the problem with me believing in the Wretched Man? If we can believe in God without persecution, why can't we believe in the devil?"

Dr. Erich crossed his arms, realizing he'd walked into a trap.

Isaac continued, "If Dr. Brady can believe that a carpenter rose from the dead, then you should let me and everyone else from Callahan believe in whatever the hell they want."

Dr. Erich looked to either side of the board for advice, receiving none. He sighed, picked up his pen and flipped to another section of Isaac's file.

"Well then, I have one question for you, Mr. Murphy. Do you believe that you are a danger to others?"

Isaac closed his eyes and his hands tightened into fists. "*Inhale. Count to five. Exhale. Count to five.*"

"My wife and daughter died because I wasn't there to save them." Isaac's knuckles turned white. "My city died because I wasn't a good enough detective." Isaac opened his bloodshot eyes. "My best friend died because I failed him in his hour of need."

Isaac gazed at the ceiling as if he could see the blue sky above. "And I almost strangled the only person left who wanted to help me." He smiled warmly. "And she forgave me."

Dr. Erich put down his pen and gazed at Isaac with grudging respect.

"You don't have to worry about me hurting myself or anyone else. I think we've all suffered enough," Isaac finished.

Dr. Erich nodded and glanced at Dr. Brady, who also nodded. Dr. Erich reached for a rubber stamp and raised it above Isaac's file. *Thump!* Approved.

***

It was late autumn. Isaac and Grace found themselves at the famous Charleston Battery sea wall. Leaning against the railing, they were looking out across the harbor and the Ravenel Bridge. Grace waved at a passing sailboat and the people aboard waved back. Winter was approaching and the lightest touch of a cold breeze ruffled Grace's long hair.

Isaac was holding a large cup of bright red strawberry gelato. There were two spoons inside, and he and Grace had been eating their fill. It was sweet and fruity.

"I used to eat this all the time. This and a praline - oh my God," Grace exclaimed, through a mouthful of gelato.

Isaac chuckled and glanced at a pair of tweeting birds who had landed on the railing. His hair was neatly trimmed and short and he looked better now than he had in nearly a year.

"Was it nice to grow up in Charleston? Because I've really enjoyed my visit," he said.

Grace beamed. "Of course! This place is magic. Nobody leaves once they live here. Well, maybe the stupid ones."

"Ah, so you?" Isaac teased.

Grace rolled her eyes. "I walked into that one! But yeah, it's a lovely city. My folks used to take my sister and I out on our sailboat. We'd sail up and down the harbor and even did some fishing farther out in the ocean. Mom was an expert sailor."

Isaac closed his eyes and tried to imagine a childhood on the water.

"You know, maybe once things get situated, I'll move down here with Amy. Get a house out in the suburbs, let Amy grow up with a bunch of kids. She shouldn't have to spend another day in Callahan."

Grace smiled but a twinge of concern flickered in her eyes.

"So, it's been cleared then? The custody?" she asked.

Isaac crossed his arms. "Well, I've been over it with David's lawyer and mine. With both Charlotte and David deceased, whatever custody battle they were fighting became irrelevant. Their will supersedes everything else, and it named me Amy's guardian. David's brother, Kevin, also had no interest in custody."

Grace gave him a sympathetic look.

"It wasn't your fault about David," she promised.

Isaac changed the subject. "I pick her up from child services next week. Thanks to the governor's bill - thanks to you - my record is clear. I can legally adopt."

"I'm really happy for you," she beamed. Isaac looked at his hands, still troubled.

"What is it?" Grace asked.

"It bothers me that they've rustled up a bunch of the anarchist leaders and labeled them as the Ghost Killers. It's true that some were violent – even killers – but they aren't at fault for all those murders. They're just scapegoats for the government and media," Isaac spat.

Grace's eyes darkened. "They had to put the blame on someone. Someone had to take the fall."

Isaac shook his head, remembering Emily's final moments.

"I couldn't save Callahan. I failed Emily."

Grace gave him a reassuring pat on the shoulder.

"Remember what I said that night? Maybe it was never about saving the city. A city is just a place. It's the people inside who matter. And you saved me the night Callahan burned. And you will save Amy."

Isaac sighed and looked off to the north. It was hundreds of miles away, but he could still feel the evil of the Bobbit Rock.

"I didn't stop the hatred. So, Callahan died."

Isaac pushed away from the railing.

"Once I pick up Amy, I'll make us all dinner," he added.

Grace reacted to a certain tone in his voice.

"What's up?" she asked, worried.

"I'm going back to the Bobbit Rock, to put an end to this."

"Oh, Isaac," she said, devastated.

Isaac cut her off with a hug.

"Thank you," he whispered.

"For what?"

"For staying with me to the end."

***

The sun was just rising as Isaac passed by the Callahan exit. His phone rang, suddenly. Perplexed, he checked the number.

"What the," he muttered, raising it to his ear.

"Austin?" he asked, surprised. There was a pause, then the Beaufort twang of Austin's accent responded.

"Hey, Isaac. I'm glad you got out."

"I did. And I heard you were alive. What's up?"

There was another pause, and, in the background, Isaac heard someone barking orders.

"Well, you know they're executing the 'Ghost Killers' today, right?"

"Yeah, to cover their own asses."

More orders being yelled could be heard.

"Jesus, what's happening over there?" Isaac exclaimed.

Austin didn't respond immediately, but Isaac could hear him moving somewhere quieter as the voices faded.

"It's a shitshow here," Austin said. "The corruption is unbelievable. Conspiracies are rampant and word is leaking out. Big government names are involved. It's really sketchy. Since I was one of the last officers on the force the night Callahan burned, I've been ordered to work the execution." Austin dropped his voice to a whisper. "I figured you should know, the street name of one of the anarchists is Eight. I checked, and he's only got eight fingers and a scar on his head, looks just like the police sketch."

Isaac turned white as a sheet. The phone almost fell out of his limp hand. Isaac pulled onto the shoulder before he wrecked the rental car.

"You still there?" Austin broke the silence.

Isaac took a deep breath. "What is the point of this call?" he demanded.

"I'm saying that if you want to kill him before the noose does, get over here. They'll just replace him with somebody else in the brig. They've got a ton of anarchists. No one is going to care or know. Hell, one already got smoked last night. It's all for show. They just need bodies. It's still martial law here. Understand?"

Isaac didn't respond.

Austin swore under his breath.

"Look, you've got thirty minutes to get here. I hope you're close."

***

The "Ghost Killers" had been jailed in the basement of the Callahan municipal building. It had several holding cells inside and that was where they would spend their final days. The fire damage had been repaired and the building was now the new HQ for the National Guard.

Austin met Isaac outside and led him through a back door. They quickly headed to the basement, passing by two guards who both ignored them.

"They're turning a blind eye. After he's dead, we'll deal with disposal," Austin whispered.

"Where did they find him?" Isaac asked quietly.

"Grace presented your plan to clear out that tunnel. They sent in 100 soldiers. It didn't go smoothly, but Eight was pulled out along with several other leaders. This is all thanks to you."

Austin pulled out a small black Ruger .22 pistol with a suppressor. Isaac slipped a latex glove onto his right hand and Austin gave him the pistol.

"You've got a short window before the guards come back. They're fine turning a blind eye, but they can only do it for a few minutes. He's in Cell 7. When it's over, make sure you pick up the shell, give me the gun and walk straight out the door we came in. Don't say a word to the guards."

Isaac said nothing. He walked past Austin and headed to Cell 7.

***

At last, Isaac faced Eight.

The first thing he noticed was his mutilated hand. The pinky was entirely gone and only a small stump of the ring finger remained. Eight had been beaten badly. The National Guard had not been kind. He sported visible scars and was missing a few teeth. Lastly, Isaac noticed the long bald scar that ran down the middle of his scalp.

Eight glanced up at Isaac and Isaac felt the rage boil inside. Eight's eyes shifted to the gun in Isaac's hand. He parted his lips just a tad.

"Here we are again, Isaac. Are you going to miss like last time?" Isaac raised the pistol and pointed the muzzle at the center of Eight's forehead. Eight did not flinch.

"If that's it then," Eight whispered. He closed his eyes.

Isaac's finger touched the trigger as the fire burned inside of him.

"Save Callahan," Emily's voice whispered in Isaac's mind. The flames extinguished and Isaac's finger froze on the trigger. He struggled internally until he finally spat out,

"Why did you do it?"

Eight's eyes cracked open slowly.

"This can be my confessional, then. Every man should confess his sins before his death," he muttered, casting a blank gaze at Isaac, ignoring the pistol.

"I did it because I wanted to feel something. Killing is just like dope. You're always chasing that first high, and you can never reach it again. So, I killed in more and more... depraved ways to up the thrill – increase the dosage. I hadn't killed a pregnant woman before. That was certainly a new spin on an old game. I always did my work professionally so I could never be traced. I wore gloves, masks, burned the clothes after... you get the point."

Eight pointed at Isaac's gun with his mutilated hand.

"I marked you two at the grocery one day, followed you home. I knew you were the problem - always strapped. But that made it a challenge. Made it fun again. So, I strapped on some body armor, because I knew there were guns in that house. Then, I waited until you left for work. I got high first, then pushed in. Of course, you came back in the middle." Eight glanced at his hand.

"It's funny. The pain I felt that day was higher than anything I'd ever experienced. I thank you for that. It made me feel truly alive for the first time in so long." Eight blinked and wiggled his stump of a ring finger.

"Killing your wife and baby didn't make me feel much. But that pain,"

Isaac nodded; this was not what he expected.

"What made you like this?" he asked.

Eight chuckled, but the laugh was void of any emotion. He was just going through the motions.

"I'm not delving into my childhood. Maybe I went to bed hungry and bloody every night. Or maybe I was a spoiled brat who got everything he ever wanted. It doesn't matter. What matters is that in time, I hated myself more than anyone else could. And people did and still do hate me. That's good - I deserve it." Eight looked at the cold floor and sighed.

"I really hope God is real. Because if after all this, there's nothing but a black void when I die, that would be a bit of letdown. It'd be much more satisfactory for hell to be hot then for it to be nothing at all. I figure I deserve at least that much for what I've done." Eight shrugged.

"I've killed. I've raped. I've tortured. And I've always been careful about it. Covered my tracks. Like a ghost." Eight sighed and continued, "There's a billion more like me. Humanity is wretched. I am wretched. *We* are the Wretched Man."

Isaac looked at the space above Eight's shoulders and grimaced. Eight pointed at the pistol.

"Go ahead. Get on with it." Eight closed his eyes again.

Isaac lowered the pistol.

"I forgive you."

Eight's eyes snapped open in shock. He stared at Isaac, stunned. Isaac met his stare. Eight tried to say something, but for the first time, he was at a loss for words. Isaac turned heel and walked away from the cell, leaving Eight alone.

***

A small number of witnesses were permitted to observe the execution, along with some military brass, politicians, Governor Randall and the remnants of the Callahan PD.

The five "Ghost Killers" would be hung by the neck until dead. The order was given, and the culprits were led out onto the platform.

Eight searched the crowd and found Isaac at the front. The two locked eyes.

A noose was placed around Eight's neck. A blindfold was offered, but he refused, keeping his gaze square with Isaac's. The two didn't waver as the last rites were given. The executioner placed his hand on the lever.

Eight mouthed to Isaac, "You saved me."

The lever was pulled, and the Ghost Killers were dropped. Eight held his gaze with Isaac's all the way down.

***

Isaac stepped up to his front door. He pulled out his keys while letting out a slow, calming breath. Unlocking the door, he stepped inside and paused at the threshold to gaze around at the clean interior. Grace had stopped by occasionally to keep things nice, knowing Isaac would return eventually.

He dropped his things off and walked up to the bedroom. Once inside, he glanced at the portrait of Emily and smiled.

"Alright, baby girl," he whispered. He squared his shoulders and walked into the hallway, stopping at the entrance to the attic. He reached up to the folding attic stairs and pulled them down via a hanging line. The stairs opened with a few puffs of dust. Isaac carefully climbed up to the attic and looked around.

"There," he muttered, searching in a corner. He opened a large trunk filled with mementos and souvenirs of his childhood, from photos to school awards and favorite comic books. He pulled out a picture of Emily and him at senior prom. Isaac's hair was slicked back and Emily was nervous in her first strapless dress. Isaac chuckled.

Within an hour, Isaac had framed and hung several childhood photos throughout the house. He looked with satisfaction at a photo of him at 7 climbing a tree. There was also a photo of him playing cops and robbers with David. But his favorite photo was of Emily when she was 12, chip-toothed and still a tomboy. For so long he'd tried to keep his childhood hidden away because of the taint of the Wretched Man.

After redecorating, Isaac went to the nursery and opened the door. He bit his lip and looked around at the beautiful nursery. He gazed at the crib which would never be used.

"Amy's bed can go right there," he said. He started to clear out the nursery, moving some of the more infant stuff out of the way, but keeping all the stuffed animals and other toys.

"What else should I get her? I know David wanted her to do music so maybe I'll get her a-" Something in the corner caught Isaac's eye. He stopped speculating and took a closer look. It was a photo of his mother and father.

"I didn't put that there," Isaac muttered. He approached the picture, which was sitting on the windowsill. It was dust free. Isaac lifted it.

"Emily," Isaac whispered with a smile.

***

Isaac withdrew the sketch of the Wretched Man's face from the safe. He gazed at his own eyes that he had drawn inside the sockets. Shaking his head, he brought it downstairs and grabbed a pencil. He grabbed a fresh sheaf of paper and set to work on a new drawing. Without a shake or a tremble, he perfectly drew the face of the devil. Once finished, he stared at the face unflinchingly.

In his office, he made a dozen copies of it then folded them into a dozen envelopes. He went to his computer and typed out a statement.

This is the face of the Wretched Man. Look at it and do not be afraid. Please spread this picture as far and wide as you can. Be not afraid of what you can see.

Isaac printed a dozen statements and slipped them into the envelopes He attached postage and addressed them to various news stations and newspapers in South Carolina. Satisfied, he prepared to mail them out.

***

Isaac pulled onto the shoulder and parked the rental car. The tree line lay directly ahead. He checked but saw no one along the road. A chilly breeze rustled through the dead forest leaves, making Isaac button up his coat.

If he listened, he could almost hear the sounds of his youth, the kids playing, racing and laughing. He was sure that if he paid close enough attention, he'd hear Emily teasing him about his bike-riding skill. Isaac smiled wistfully.

Isaac started down the trail. It would be a long hike. But he knew it by heart, going just once to the Bobbit Rock was more than enough to have it etched into his memory.

Isaac stepped off the trail and into the thick forest. Sunlight nearly vanished under the thick canopy, plunging Isaac into a world of shadows. The only sounds were the crunching of leaves under his boots and the faint wail of a lonesome wind through the branches.

The hairs on the back of his neck rose as he approached the clearing. *"Inhale. Count to five. Exhale. Count to five."*

His feet automatically carried him forward into the dead clearing. Isaac raised his gaze and stared at the Bobbit Rock. It had been two decades since he last stood in its presence. But he had seen the rock in his dreams every night since.

Isaac approached the rock and tightened up the strap on his rucksack. He reached out to place a foot on the first step. *"One more time. For me, for Amy and for a new life."*

The last time he climbed the rock, it was because of rage. This time, he climbed the rock for love. He hoisted himself through the air and scaled the sheer face effortlessly. There was no fear. There was no worry. He reached the Leap, not even daunted by the drop to the sharp rocks below.

"Alright." He reached into his rucksack and withdrew a folding knife. Wincing, he made a small cut on his forearm. He smeared the blood against the rock face as a sacrifice. Once done, he pulled out a bandage and quickly wrapped up the cut. He tossed the rucksack back over his shoulders and stepped up to the jump.

Isaac jumped.

He stuck to the sheer face like a spider and shimmied up to the top. Throwing his hands over the lip, he pulled himself onto the plateau. He planted his feet on the rock and stood, big and tall, in the sky. He gazed at the gorgeous Appalachian Mountains. From this height, he could see for miles in all directions. The clearing didn't seem so awful - how could it when it was surrounded by so much life?

Exhilarated, Isaac turned his gaze to the heavens and took a deep breath. The air rushed into his lungs and he held it as long as he could. With arms stretched wide, he let it go with a shout of exaltation.

Without fear, he faced the Wretched Man.

"I am not afraid of you. You cannot hurt me. So, you can stay on my shoulders if you want, until the die I day if you like. But you will get *nothing* from me. Away with you."

Isaac turned his back on the devil and began the climb down. He reached the bottom, where Emily was waiting.

She was curled up at the base of the rock. Isaac knelt and nestled in close to her. In Emily's arms was baby Samantha. She had fine blonde hair and big twinkling green eyes. Emily held her finger next to Samantha's face. Samantha giggled and took it with a tiny hand.

"Are you ready?" Emily asked.

A tear rolled down Isaac's cheek. "Yes," he whispered, his throat tightening up. He gazed at Samantha and smiled through the tears.

Emily took his hand in hers and kissed it. "I love you. I always will," she murmured.

"I love you, too. And I always will," Isaac affirmed.

Emily ran her fingers through Samantha's shining hair.

"I'm so proud of you. You kept your promise," she said.

Isaac looked at Emily's angelic face.

"Not in the way I thought," he replied.

Emily smiled at him. "You're a wonderful man. And a wonderful father. You'll be everything to Amy, I know you will."

Isaac kissed Emily in the nape of her neck.

"I'm going to miss you so much," he whispered. Emily returned the kiss. "One day you'll be with us again. But right now, she needs you."

Isaac wiped his eyes and nodded.

"I know. I'll be the father to her that I would have been to Samantha."

Isaac embraced Emily and Samantha raised her chubby arms out to him.

"Would you like to hold her?" Emily asked.

Isaac nodded, holding out his hands. He nuzzled his daughter to his chest.

"Hi, Samantha. You are so beautiful, aren't you, sweet baby?" Isaac kissed Samantha on the forehead, and then just looked at her, trying to absorb every wonderful detail.

"She has my eyes," he murmured. Samantha giggled.

"And your smile," Emily added.

Emily leaned forward and took Isaac's face into her hands.

"Go now. Amy needs you."

"Goodbye, my two loves," Isaac whispered.

Emily leaned forward and kissed him tenderly. Isaac closed his eyes and returned it. When he opened his eyes, he was alone once more. This time however, there was no anguish. There was no anger. There was no fear. He had hope.

He reached into his rucksack and withdrew the portrait of Emily. He placed it at the base of the Bobbit Rock and then turned away. The Bobbit Rock had caused so much misery. Now, it would only ever be a source of love from the woman Isaac had always cherished.

The sun poked through the clouds and bathed the clearing in a warm golden glow. Isaac smelled the rich forest and pure *life* around him. As Isaac left for Amy, Emily's portrait reflected a glint of sunlight and shined brightly.

BOBBIT ROCK

10. AMY

Isaac and Grace sat in the courthouse together, waiting for his name to be called. He glanced at her, and she smiled encouragingly. Footsteps echoed in the distance.

"God, I'm nervous," Isaac confessed.

"Don't be. She's going to be so happy to see you."

Isaac looked up at his Child Protective Services caseworker as she stopped in front of them.

"Isaac, it's time! Follow me and I'll take you to her," she said with a smile.

Grace gave Isaac a reassuring pat on the knee. "Go on. I'll wait here,"

Isaac took a deep breath and rose to his feet, a little shaky, but determined, nonetheless. "Okay. I'm ready." He followed the caseworker down the hallway as she spoke.

"Amy has been talking nonstop about how excited she is to go home with you. It has really helped her with the coping. Nothing is more rewarding than seeing kids who've been through a tragedy find joy," the caseworker beamed.

Isaac nodded, unable to find a response. They stopped in front of a playroom.

"And here we are...." The caseworker opened the door and stepped inside. Isaac froze for just a second. The slightest twinge of dread crept up his spine.

He looked left. Clear. He looked right. Clear. He looked up....

Isaac stared at the space above him for just a second. He then looked forward.

"Uncle Isaac!" Amy shouted with glee. She rushed toward Isaac, who grinned and swung her up into his arms.

"Oh, my! Look how big you've gotten! What have they been feeding you?" Isaac asked as he lifted her above his head. Amy giggled happily.

Isaac grinned and placed Amy on his shoulders.

"Wow! I can see so much from up here, Uncle Isaac!"

"Come on, little angel. Let's go home."

Acknowledgements

First off, I would like to thank my wonderful editor, Leslie Mizell. I wish to extend my thanks to Shilah LaCoe and Kathy Meis at Bublish for their help in publishing this story. A heartfelt thanks also goes out to my parents for their love and support. I want to thank Joe Gatta for giving me insight on the story when it was a script. I also want to thank Rouslan Ovtcharoff for his insight and help in getting the script professionally reviewed. I want to thank my grandparents for their amazing support. I also thank Margaret LeVan Dominguez for her amazing artistry on the cover. Lastly, I want to thank Barry Yeoman for his mentorship at Duke Young Writer's Camp.

CPSIA information can be obtained
at www.ICGtesting.com
Printed in the USA
LVHW032017081019
633405LV00003B/1057/P